I0762953

WE BURNED SO BRIGHT

ALSO BY TJ KLUNE
FROM TOR PUBLISHING GROUP

BOOKS FOR ADULTS

The Green Creek Series

Wolfsong

Ravensong

Heartsong

Brothersong

The Cerulean Chronicles

The House in the Cerulean Sea

Somewhere Beyond the Sea

Standalones

The Bones Beneath My Skin

Under the Whispering Door

In the Lives of Puppets

BOOKS FOR YOUNG ADULTS

The Extraordinaries Series

The Extraordinaries

Flash Fire

Heat Wave

WE BURNED SO BRIGHT

TJ KLUNE

TOR PUBLISHING GROUP

NEW YORK

This is a work of fiction. All of the names, characters, organizations, places, and events portrayed in this work are either products of the author's imagination or used fictitiously.

WE BURNED SO BRIGHT

A Tor Book
Published by Tom Doherty Associates / Tor Publishing Group
120 Broadway
New York, NY 10271

www.torpublishinggroup.com

Tor® is a registered trademark of Macmillan Publishing Group, LLC.

EU Representative: Macmillan Publishers Ireland Ltd, 1st Floor, The Liffey Trust Centre, 117–126 Sheriff Street Upper, Dublin 1, D01 YC43

The Library of Congress Cataloging-in-Publication Data is available upon request.

ISBN 978-1-250-88123-6 (hardcover)
ISBN 978-1-250-44642-8 (international, sold outside the U.S., subject to rights availability)
ISBN 978-1-250-88124-3 (ebook)

First Edition: 2026

Printed in the United States of America

10 9 8 7 6 5 4 3 2 1

For my editor, Ali Fisher,
whose little note sparked the idea for this book.

And to NB and TJB,
for making it through the darkness.

Author's Note

This story explores love and grief at the end of the world.

There are discussions of death in different forms, including death by suicide.

Please read with care.

CHAPTER 1

Don switched off the television. He'd spent the morning in the garden, those pesky weeds returning with a vengeance. All that spring rain, he thought. And for what?

His husband, Rodney, sat in a recliner a few feet away. At seventy-eight, Rodney was a gruff and quiet man, his bushy eyebrows doing most of the talking for him. Forty years together, and Don could tell what he was thinking without a word between them.

"I know," Don said. "It's time."

Rodney grunted in response, leaning forward in his chair, hands on his knees. His back was bothering him, though he wouldn't say as much. But Don knew. Of course he did. He knew everything about Rodney. Rodney, who looked over at Don, expression softening. "You all right?"

"No, I don't think I am."

Rodney nodded and stood from the recliner, groaning as he did so, knees popping. "Stay right there," he said.

Don did, staring off into nothing. He didn't know how to feel. Frightened? Oh yes. Angry? Perhaps; a little spark that whispered *how is this fair?*

But mostly, Don felt relieved, and oddly so. Not over the fact that the entire world would be gone in thirty days, give or take. No, he wasn't the type to revel in the misfortune of others. His relief came in knowing how it would end.

Getting older meant he was running down the clock as it was, thoughts sometimes straying to darker corners:

Would it be the colon?

The heart?

A little pop in a blood vessel of the brain that caused one to drop dead?

The human body was a miracle that was not meant to last. He felt it in the stiffening of his joints. Stretch wrong in the morning? That was a week's worth of discomfort. Get a blood test? Ooh, what could be found in *that*?

Now, though. Now, it was different. Now, the mystery of death—*when, how, why*—was solved for everyone.

Rodney returned. Don didn't know how long he'd been gone. He carried a small box with him—oak polished within an inch of its life, a brass keyhole in the front. Roughly the size of a jewelry box, it wasn't large nor was it heavy, but Rodney was careful with it.

He said, "If we're going to do this, we have to do it now."

Don lowered his head. "I know. It's . . . You always think there's going to be more time."

"We have enough," Rodney said. "That's what counts."

Don looked out the window. Clouds in the sky, wispy clouds that stretched above a green forest. The sun, shining. Birds singing. And if the people who knew about these things were right, all of it would be gone in a month. Either the planet would be cracked apart, chunks of rock being pulled toward infinity, or it would be stretched and stretched and stretched until the entire world was a thin, straight line, unable to support life.

The cause? A rogue black hole. A one-in-a-trillion chance, they'd been told breathlessly. There was a one-in-a-trillion chance a black hole would find its way to our little corner of the universe. Astronomical odds, and yet, now a reality.

Which meant chaos, of course. Military vehicles in the streets of most cities and towns. Looting, rioting, the burning of cars and buildings and people, all of it had already happened. They'd known about the black hole for close to a year, and in those early days, more things were aflame than not. When backed into a corner, an animal could be dangerous. Humans were animals, and deadly ones at that.

Over the last year, they'd proven themselves as such. In Arizona, a group of people had doused themselves in gasoline. As a horrified crowd looked on, someone flicked a lighter, and up they went in fire and smoke, all in the name of leaving the world behind on their own terms. In Nebraska, thirty-four people attempted to take the capitol, but ten of them were shot before they could get inside. Six died from their injuries. In Paris, massive crowds filled the streets, storefront windows shattered as people looted everything that wasn't bolted down. In Cape Town, hundreds of people walked into the ocean and drowned. Some held children. Others assisted the elderly. In Chengdu, dozens of people leapt from the tops of skyscrapers while others looked on with blank expressions, waiting their turn. In Denmark, a self-proclaimed prophet said that before the planet was destroyed, Heaven would open up for the chosen, and they would rise into Eternal Glory. He amassed crowds in the thousands, his voice carrying over a packed field. During one of his pulpit sessions, he was stabbed to death by a woman who cried as she raised and lowered the knife again and again. No one tried to stop her until it was already too late. The prophet died choking on his own blood. The woman—older, shouting and screaming—did not resist when the crowd descended upon her.

"We'll be careful," Don said, gaze going back to the chest in Rodney's arms. "Take the back roads. Avoid major freeways."

"When?" Rodney asked.

"Tomorrow."

And so it was decided.

When they'd retired ten years ago, it'd been unexpected. Both had planned to work a few more years, but then life happened, and both were pulled away in a direction they hadn't expected. Rodney had worked for the state in a thankless role, filling out endless reports for any little thing the government could think of. Don had managed the office for a physical therapist, doing so for damn near fifteen years. And then . . . well. An ending, of sorts, one they had both expected and dreaded in equal measure. Cut off, like a limb had been removed without discussion.

Seven months in, Rodney had bought an RV.

Don had not been pleased.

Their friends—all older—had been excited. RV life was a different breed, they said. Why, buying their own RVs had been one of the best decisions they had ever made for themselves. A hotel on wheels! Sure, you had to find a place to park for the night—avoid Walmarts if you could—but there were so many places made for RVs. Hell, there were thousands upon thousands of retirees who'd done the same and hadn't regretted it.

Yes, it would be grand, except the RV was an ugly thing: old, with dented siding and rust around the wheel wells. White, with a fat dirt-brown line down the sides. Not one of the overpriced RVs that looked and traveled like a bus. No, this one was more akin to a camper slapped onto an old truck. But its worst sin was a set of hideous brown-and-pink knitted blinds that hung in the small bedroom. Don was not a fan of those blinds.

Small wonders, the RV ran, belching out thick black exhaust from the tailpipe. Registered, passed inspection (barely), and guzzled gas like it was an endless pit. But Rodney was charmed by it, saying he thought they could get on the road, taking in sights and people they'd never had the time to see before. Don had never really considered himself an RV person, but he could picture it in his mind: long summer days with nothing but the open road, the sun setting in the distance, making the sky pink and red and orange. An audiobook on the radio, one he'd always meant to get to, but hadn't had the time.

He often thought about that: time. How interminable it could be, and then in a blink of an eye, years have gone by.

Oh, the places they'd gone: To Montana and water so clear, the deep lakebeds looked within arm's reach. To Arizona, standing before the Grand Canyon, the rock burnt red, the air sizzling hot. To the Appalachian Trail, hiking a good eight miles before calling it quits. To Wyoming, the Grand Tetons rising in all their majesty. To Utah, the petrified forest, rocks in impossible hues. To Tennessee and the Great Smoky Mountains, trying to reach the top of Mount Le Conte.

Years of travel, years of doing what needed to be done. And now, at last, the trip they'd been putting off because that made the distance *real*, something they'd long avoided. They had no other choice.

Don was seventy-two years old.

It took them longer than expected to pack up the RV. An entire lifetime of trinkets and memories to leave behind, all contained within the walls of a home Don had thought would be their last. Thirty-odd years ago, they'd seen it for the first time, their Realtor chattering away about the curb appeal, the original wood floors, the updated bathrooms. They'd thought on it for a few days—seen some other houses, too—but kept coming back to it. The wood siding, the brick base. The apple tree in the backyard. The trees surrounding them, the nearest neighbor half a mile away. Eventually, it was theirs, and they'd made a home out of it, filled with friends and hope and fights and tears and laughter.

Rodney and Don stood in front of the house, hands clasped between them. *A lovely man*, Don thought to himself, even as he shivered and wiped a stray tear from his cheek. This was harder than he'd thought it'd be. He wondered how many other people were doing the same thing they were, right at this very moment. Saying goodbye to their homes for one last adventure before it was all over.

"It's not all bad," Rodney said abruptly, in that way he did when his emotions were too big.

"It isn't?"

"No."

"How do you figure?"

"I don't know," he admitted. "But we still have the chance to . . ." He trailed off.

Don knew what he was trying to say, even if he couldn't finish. "To apologize. To be there for him."

Rodney didn't look at him. "Yeah. Yes. That."

Friends came to see them off on a drizzly spring day. Tears were shed. They told each other that it wasn't goodbye, it wasn't the end, but rather, it was so long, see you later, alligator. These were lies, of course; though they didn't say as much, everyone knew this would be the last time they'd be together like this.

Tina and her husband, Craig, brought them muffins in a plastic container. She said they were lemon poppyseed. They looked half-baked, gritty.

Jim—their elderly neighbor who often complained about everything to anyone who would listen—told them they were foolish. Going on the road was a death sentence. Dumbasses, he called them, before waving and going back to his house.

Ernest and June, an attractive couple in their midfifties, stopped by shortly before they left. June was crying quietly, a tissue balled up in her hands. She spoke only briefly, saying, "Tell him . . . tell him we said hello. And goodbye." And then she buried her face in her hands.

"You sure about this?" Ernest asked Rodney. "Heard some crazy things are going on out there. I know how important this is, but . . ."

"We're sure," Rodney said simply.

But Ernest wasn't finished. "Two older men on the road. You need to be careful, Rodney. There are people out there who will try and take advantage of you."

Rodney snorted. "I'd like to see them try."

They hugged and made promises that they could not keep. Standing side by side on the walkway leading up to their house, they watched as their friends and neighbors returned to their homes.

Eventually, Rodney said, "We're wasting time."

"Yes," Don whispered.

They sat in the RV, staring at the house. Behind them, tucked neatly away on a shelf, the wooden box. Don waited for Rodney to start the RV. He didn't.

Instead, his hands shook.

Don said, "When we first saw this house, I told myself, isn't that nice? I could picture it, you know. Even then. Our life. Together. Here, in this place. It'd be a good life, I thought. For all of us. Christmases. Birthdays."

"It was," Rodney said, gripping the steering wheel so tightly his knuckles turned white. "A good life. The best life."

Well, no. It wasn't, it couldn't be. But if Rodney needed that white lie to push himself forward, Don wasn't going to take it from him. Not now. Not yet.

"It was, wasn't it," Don said. "Even with everything."

"Even with everything," Rodney agreed.

When they'd bought the house, the flower beds had been mostly barren aside from a few scraggly hedges that hadn't been trimmed in who knew how long. Don'd spent years getting it right.

First, he rebuilt the flower beds on his own. Dug out all the dirt, the plastic sheeting, the miles and miles of roots. Brought in fresh, nutrient-rich soil. Planted flowers in every color he could think of. Out in the back, he'd sectioned off an area along the fence to the right. Tore up that part of the yard. Put in small trees and strawberries and blueberries and carrots and vines that grew and grew and grew until they crawled up the fence.

Rodney helped, sometimes, but Don loved doing it on his own. It was *his* thing, something he hadn't been very good at to start, but had learned along the way. It took time, Don said, gardening did. Patience. A willingness to be wrong and have to start all over again.

Plants were, in his estimation, as finicky as people could be, and just as dramatic. Prune a plant the wrong way, and it'd die just to prove a point.

"What will you miss?" he asked his husband.

Rodney's hands relaxed on the steering wheel. "Mornings," he finally said. "When it's cool outside. Dew on the grass, looking like diamonds when the morning sunlight shines upon them. A low fog that'll burn off by nine. It's quiet, then. So very quiet. People don't appreciate mornings, and for good reason. We have to get up to go to school. To work. To meetings and appointments. I spent my whole life not seeing what a morning looks like. After retirement, it was like I was seeing it again for the first time." He paused. Then, "It's going to hurt."

Don closed his eyes. "I know. But we made a promise to ourselves. To be there for him. And besides, how much more can it hurt? We've already been through the worst. In all honesty, it . . ." He paused, then forced himself through the rest. "I think we need to go and say what needs to be said. Both of us."

Rodney didn't respond. A moment later, the RV grumbled to life, and they left their home behind for the last time.

CHAPTER 2

They headed west, chasing after the setting sun. Avoid major highways, avoid major cities. Might as well avoid Johnny Law as best they could. They had enough food to last them until the end. Extra gas in plastic containers. Flashlights, blankets, a basin to wash clothes in if they couldn't find a laundromat. A small generator should it be needed. Don tried eating one of the muffins, but he couldn't choke it down.

By the time they were on the road—their home shrinking behind them—Don was dry-eyed and clearheaded. The reality of their situation was not lost on him. But he wasn't alone. Everyone in the world was going through something similar. For perhaps the first time in history, the entirety of civilization knew the same thing: It was only a matter of time.

They left the safety of Camden, Maine, for the unknown world beyond. They passed children playing in yards, mothers holding babies as they played in sprinklers. A sign in front of one house read REPENT WHILE YOU STILL CAN! The smell of Atlantic salt water was thick as ever.

The roads were packed. People with the same idea, to get away, away. As if any distance would matter. But Rodney was a Maine native. He knew the back roads, the secret paths that wound through the trees. Others did too, but not so many.

They didn't speak much, at least not at first, both lost in their own little worlds. Rodney had his hands at ten and two on the steering wheel, hunched forward slightly and squinting as if his glasses weren't sitting on the dashboard in front of him.

Don, though, Don was in his head. Don was thinking about the first time they'd met. Don was thinking about the way Rodney had appeared, as if by magic. At a coffee shop, packed with people. Don had only found a table after watching like a hawk. He'd waited until the people sitting at one had finished, stood up, and then swooped in to claim it for himself.

Breakfast tea with sugar and a dollop of milk. A flaky croissant that melted on his tongue. An open book with thousands of words left to read.

And then Rodney had been there, standing above the table, coffee in hand. He said, "Mind if I sit here? No other spots."

Though irritated, Don said, "Fine, fine," as he made room. Rodney—though Don did not know his name yet—nodded and sat.

The conversation that arose due to proximity was forced at first, awkward pleasantries coming in fits and starts. But it smoothed out after a time, and Don was strangely enchanted by this man. Rodney, he was called. Rodney with his slate-colored eyes, and the devastating way he could arch his eyebrow. Don didn't think he'd ever laughed as much before then, and by the time they were finished, Don thought he'd met someone worth knowing.

It took them almost two weeks to see each other again. This time, for dinner, one where they were so caught up in conversation that they didn't see the restaurant closing down around them. They kissed once that night, a bare scrape of lips, hidden in the shadows of the parking lot. Three days later, Rodney had spent the night. That was forty years ago. He'd never left.

Don looked over at him now and said, "I think about you all the time."

Rodney grunted. "I'm right here."

"I know. But still."

Rodney stared straight ahead. "What should we say?" He coughed, clearing his throat. "When we get there. To him."

"Everything," Don said, though he was careful about it. Dangerous ground, this. "We hold nothing back."

"Right," Rodney said gruffly.

Don said, "I think about you. Your face. Your eyes. Your mind. I'm still so in love with you."

"I know," Rodney said.

They took their time, stopping to get pictures of deer in the woods, of long, lonely windswept fields, knowing that no one would ever see them. But it felt . . . normal. Habitual. They stood under a tall tree and looked up, marveling at how high it seemed to go. Rodney found a patch of irises growing along a dirt road and touched their petals with his callused hands. Little things that might have meant nothing the day before had taken on new meaning. Those first few days, they ate outside, sitting at a park table or in lawn chairs they'd brought with them. Looking up at the sun, the moon, the clouds, the stars.

They found others like them. Others who had packed up their entire lives, though few of them had a destination in mind. Families in cars. People in RVs like theirs. People in RVs much nicer than theirs. People who had quit their jobs, pulled their kids out of school, all in the name of finding some sort of meaning, an explanation.

"It's like cancer," one man told them both. "You look fine on the outside, but it's a lie, one that'll catch up to you sooner than you think."

His partner—a young lady with frizzy hair—said, "I think we're the cancer, and this is a way to course-correct."

The man snorted but did not speak.

She ignored him. "Think about it. What happens when the body senses an invading force? It does everything it can to stop it. Maybe this is just the universe's way of deciding we're an infection that needs to be stopped." She smiled a terrible smile. "It's almost the same, really. All that radiation we'll feel."

She began to cry. The man apologized, and led her away back to their own camp.

Don said, "I used to think about it more."

"What?" Rodney asked, staring off into the encroaching darkness.

"Dying. I used to think about it all the time. Now, not so much. Isn't that funny?"

Rodney looked at him.

Don stared back.

When they laughed, it was a quiet thing.

It was in Vermont that they met the family.

Driving along a two-lane highway, Patsy Cline on the radio, the sky outside thick with clouds. Don was dozing slightly, head against the window. Then the RV began to rattle around them, and Rodney cursed. Don shot up, mind hazy, his first clear thought that the end had come sooner than anyone had expected.

The steering wheel jerked left, then right, and they came to a stop at an angle, the RV groaning around them.

"What happened?" Don asked, heart thudding in his chest.

"Flat tire," Rodney said, slapping the steering wheel. "Of all the—You all right?"

"Startled me, is all. You?"

Rodney laughed, a mixture of relief and annoyance. "Yeah, I'm fine." He flexed his hands against the steering wheel. "Always something, isn't it?"

"Well, get off the road. Don't want to be blocking it when more people come."

He did as he was told. Carefully, he pulled the limping RV off to the side onto a little dirt pullout. After switching the RV off, Rodney clambered out, muttering under his breath. Don followed and found Rodney glaring at the left rear tire.

"Picked up a nail," he said. "See it?"

Don did. Near the top, in the middle. The tire itself wasn't in too bad condition—some tread left—but the nail was firmly embedded, air hissing out around it. "The spare?"

"Checked it before I bought it. Not a donut, so we should be fine. Jack is brand new."

"I'll help."

"I know you will. Come on. Let's get it done. Already losing daylight."

It took them the better part of an hour. Only a few cars drove by, no one stopping to offer assistance, not that Rodney would have accepted it. He was a proud man, for better or worse. Always wanting to do things his own way. Don loved that about him, for the most part; there were times when he'd had to put his foot down, and Rodney usually listened. He was, after all, the voice of reason. Rodney had told him that many times over the years.

By the time they'd finished, both were sore and sweaty. Cranky too, until Don reminded Rodney that in the grand scheme of things, it didn't matter. In due time, the audacity of a flat tire wouldn't be something to concern themselves with. *None of us will be here.*

It should have frightened him, that thought. It did, but nowhere near to the extent he thought it would. Perhaps that would come later, in the days ahead as time grew shorter. But here, now, in a forest so green it looked plastic, it was a faraway thing, the end.

But that was a lie. Don knew as well as anyone that time did not stop for pretty things in nature. To distract himself, he said, "No one can change a tire like you. I'm impressed."

Rodney chuckled, a slight, breathy sound. That was followed by laughter, bright and loud. Don joined in, and the two hung on to each other, laughing, laughing.

It was how the family found them, laughing and hugging and living.

They pulled away, but only just, Rodney's hand in Don's. The minivan parked right behind the RV, and a middle-aged man hung his head out the driver's-side window. "You folks okay?"

Rodney—ever the protector—squeezed Don's hand in a silent warning. He said, "We're good. Just had some nail trouble."

Three other faces stared out at them from the minivan. A woman in the passenger seat. Two children—a boy and girl—leaning between the front seats. The woman said something to the man, and he nodded along. The minivan turned off. The man stepped out.

He was short, with black hair, and looked like a dad on vacation: button-down shirt tucked into khaki cargo shorts. He had on Birkenstocks with white socks that rose halfway up his calves. He stretched, arms above his head, as the other doors to the minivan opened, kids spilling out. The man was smiling, a wide, brittle thing as if the edges of his lips were being pulled up by strings. Not warm, but not frostbitten, either. Just . . . odd.

The woman told the children to stay close by, and they headed for the trees, the boy chasing after the girl. Small, both of them, the boy probably eight or nine, the girl a couple of years younger. They stopped under a large tree and began picking up leaves from the ground.

The woman joined the man out in front of the minivan. She

wasn't smiling, instead rubbing her hands together as if cold. She looked exhausted, dark circles under her eyes, her long hair tied up in a messy bun.

The man said, "Name's John. That's my wife, Megan. Boy is Jamie. Daughter's named Lauren."

"Don," he said with an awkward wave. "My husband, Rodney."

Rodney grunted in greeting and a tip of his head, hand still in Don's. They'd heard stories. People on the road during these difficult times, not in their right minds. Robberies. Assaults. Murder. They were a family, but that didn't mean shit anymore.

John said, "What brings you folks out here?"

"Driving," Rodney said.

"On a trip," Don added.

John nodded. Megan popped her knuckles. The kids giggled as they lay on their backs on the ground.

"I hear that," John said, and Don wanted to ask him to stop smiling. It was growing uncomfortable. "Strange, isn't it?" John looked up at the sky. "Looks like it always has. Hard to believe what's coming."

Normal, this. Or, rather, the new normal. It was all anyone talked about. And why shouldn't they? It was happening to everyone. You couldn't go anywhere without someone asking what they thought about the black hole, what would happen when it finally reached Earth. Some thought it a hoax; still others believed it was God Himself, and the rapture was nigh. Don thought it was nothing but shitty, rotten luck.

"It is what it is," Rodney said. "If it wasn't one thing, it'd be another."

John laughed, a choked, wet sound. "Yeah, yeah." Then, "You think?"

Rodney shrugged. "The way I figure it, something always comes due. Can't really get around it."

"Right," John said, head bobbing up and down as if he were a marionette. "Right. Nothing much can be done. You got it in one." He looked away, rubbing a hand over his face. "Always comes due in the end."

Megan said, "We haven't told the kids." In a hurry, she added, "We will. It's just that . . ."

She didn't finish, looking at Jamie and Lauren, who by this point were pointing out shapes in the clouds.

"Pulled them out of school," John said in a low voice. "Told them we were going to take a trip of a lifetime." His throat worked. "Wanted to show them everything." He laughed to try and hide his tears. "Before it's all gone."

"Their grandparents live in Minnesota," Megan said. "That's where we're going. They live out in the middle of nowhere, and we're thinking there might be a chance."

"Right?" John asked. "You think? You think there might be a chance?"

Rodney said, "I don't know." A gentle lie.

John nodded, obviously relieved. "Okay, fine. We've been through worse before, yeah? Wars and pandemics, stuff like that. And we've always come out on top. That's what I think. I think all of this is being overblown."

Don wanted to ask: *Then why are you here? Why did you uproot your lives? Why can't you look anyone in the eye when you speak?* But he didn't. He said, "From your lips to God's ears."

The family insisted they share a meal together. A rest stop a few miles ahead had pullouts, bathrooms, grills. They found an empty stone gazebo off to one side. The rest stop was mostly empty. A couple of long-haul trucks, carrying goods that no longer mattered. A few cars. Nothing more.

Charcoal in the grill, courtesy of John. Hamburger patties from Rodney and Don. Potato chips. Soda and juice. Fruit for dessert, oranges and grapes.

The children were wary of Don and Rodney at first, but that fell away when they sat down to eat. The boy—Jamie—said that he couldn't wait for his birthday in the fall. He was going to ask for a new computer. Lauren, the little girl, showed them the rocks she'd found. One, she said, looked like a lion. She had others at home. She had to leave them behind because her mother said they didn't need to take rocks where they were going. She wondered aloud if her rocks missed her, and how she was going to wash them when she got home.

Not once did their parents correct them. Not once did their parents say they weren't going home again. That there wouldn't *be* a home left to go back to. And even if there was, odds were not in their favor that they'd live to see it again.

The parents smiled. The children laughed. Don felt like screaming.

And that only worsened when Jamie said, "Some kid at school told me we're all going to die."

John froze. Megan stiffened. Lauren grinned, a potato chip in her hand that she crushed, bits and pieces falling on the table.

"Why do you think he would say that?" Don asked after it became clear no one else would answer.

Jamie shrugged as he peeled a grape with his little fingers. "I dunno. But he said space was coming down and will make us catch on fire. Isn't that funny?"

"Kids," Megan said hoarsely. "Go play."

Jamie frowned up at her. "But I'm—"

"Now!"

They left, but they didn't go far. Every now and then, Jamie would look back at them with a confused expression. Megan ate slowly, robotically. With a mouthful of potato salad, she said, "Sorry about that. I don't know what came over me."

Don did. It was a case of the inevitabilities, and a rather serious one at that.

The meal was over, but John didn't seem quite ready to leave. He rested his elbows on the table and said, "You know, it's strange."

"What is?" Don asked, wiping his mouth with a napkin.

"This," John said. "All of this. A few hours ago, we didn't know you existed. If things were different, odds are we'd never have met. And I keep thinking, okay, it is what it is. But here you are. Here we are. Together."

"It was happenstance," Rodney said with a grunt.

John shook his head. "I don't believe that, not anymore. Not after . . . everything. I'm not saying that everything happens for a reason. But this? Here? Now? Maybe it *was* supposed to happen. Maybe we were supposed to cross paths like this."

Don didn't like the look in John's eyes. It seemed almost manic. He didn't blame John for that—how could he? But still . . . it unnerved him, being up close to someone who seemed on the verge of a breakdown.

He jumped a little when Megan said, "Where are you going?"

"West," Don said. "We're heading west."

"What's west?"

Without thinking, Don blurted, "Our son." He ignored the look Rodney shot him.

"Your son?" Megan asked. She glanced at her children, her hand at her throat. "Yes, I suppose that makes sense." Her gaze tightened. "Why isn't he with you?"

"What about after?" John asked. "Have you thought about heading north? That's what we're doing." His smile returned, lips rubbery. "You could come with us. To Minnesota. It really is the middle of nowhere. If there's a chance at surviving this thing, maybe it'll be there."

No, no it wouldn't be. Any and all land—should it remain intact and not get pulled out into space—would be scorched beyond recognition. The energy from the black hole would create tidal waves of fire so tall, nothing could stand before them and live. It didn't matter who anyone was or where they went. Billionaires in bunkers or in space. Poor people huddled in basements with dirt floors. No amount of wealth, or how good a person was, none of it mattered. They'd all meet the same end.

"We'd have more than enough room," Megan said. "I don't think anyone would mind if—"

"We can't," Don said. "Thank you for the offer, but we have something we need to see to before . . . well. Before."

"Don't you want to live?" John asked, that off look in his eyes growing brighter. "Don't you want to prove everyone wrong and survive? Think about it. This thing—whatever it is—comes. What if it misses us? What if it causes damage, but not enough to destroy the world? What if *we* could somehow continue on?"

Don could tell by the look on Rodney's face that he was almost at his limit. Don couldn't fault John for his thinking. He was reaching for something to hold on to. But Rodney . . . well. Rodney didn't suffer fools.

Don reached over and squeezed Rodney's thigh. He sighed.

"Anything is possible," Don said slowly, picking and choosing his words. "But—"

"I don't want to die," John said. "I don't want *them* to die."

"No one's dying!" Megan said shrilly. "Stop it. Just stop it. I don't want to hear about this anymore. Let's talk about something else. Flowers. Don't you just love flowers?"

"I have a garden," Don said. Not had, have. It was still there. For now. "All different varieties of blooms. I—"

"Or baseball," Megan said. "We could talk about baseball and hot dogs and those peanuts that come hot in the bag. We went to a ball game. Did you know that? About a year ago. Jamie got it in his head that he wanted to be a ballplayer. Don't know where he got that from. John doesn't like baseball, but Jamie must have seen it on TV one day, and it became his entire personality." Her smile returned. It looked like death. "He learned all the rules, the positions. Read books. Looked up things online. We got him a mitt. A bat. Took him to batting cages and wouldn't you know?" She slapped her hand against the table, causing the plastic flatware to rattle. "He was *good*. He *is* good. Has an eye. Watches the ball. Good grip on the bat. Nice swing. He has the follow-through. Fearless." A tear fell onto her cheek. "We're going to sign him up for a team next year. Get him a uniform. He already has cleats. They were so expensive. I mean, how could they cost so much? Especially for something he'll grow out of in a few months. Do you have any idea how much it costs to dress growing children? It's ridiculous!" She stood abruptly. "Sorry," she said, too loudly. "I need to run to the restroom."

Off she went, her pace hurried, shoulders hunched.

A long, drawn-out silence.

John said, "She's . . . upset."

Rodney's leg bumped against Don's. *Careful*, that movement said. *Careful.*

"Aren't we all?" Don asked. "I don't know anyone who wouldn't be—"

John grinned, gaze sharp and wet. "Yeah, of course. You're right. We should all be upset." He chuckled, a sound that seemed to crawl up his throat and out his mouth. "She's pregnant. A couple of months. We weren't planning it. Two was enough, you know? Almost too much. Jamie was a handful, and Lauren, she . . ." He blew out a breath. "She came early. Two months early. In the NICU for weeks, and I told her I'm your dad. I'm your *daddy*. And I promise you, if you pull through, if you get out of here, I will do everything in my power to make sure you get the life you deserve. I swore that to her. And guess what? She came home. It took a long time. And it was touch and go more times than I care to admit. But she persisted. She grew stronger, healthier. Still so small, but she could breathe on her own. The day we took her home? The best day of my life. I cried! I cried because *she* was crying, and I'd never heard such a crazy sound. It echoed around the house and I remember thinking, *This is it. This is what I was made for.*" John gripped the edges of the park table. "And she grew. They both did. Grew to have thoughts of their own, to have feelings about anything and everything. The two of them. From me. From Megan. We *made* them, we brought them into this world, we gave them love and hope and joy and for *what*? For this? For it all to end like this? No. No. I refuse to believe that. I refuse to believe there won't be a day when I get to see my son graduate high school. I refuse to believe there won't be a day when my daughter comes to me and says, I've met someone. I refuse to believe that my unborn kid won't get to take a breath of air. We didn't plan on it, but now that it's real, why should I let it be taken away?" He glared at them. "I have hope, but it feels like lying."

They sat in silence, only interrupted by the sounds of Jamie, of Lauren, screeching toward the sky.

Don excused himself as Rodney and John began clearing up the remnants of their meal. He wanted to use the restroom before they got back on the road. The kids were eating grapes, tossing them up and trying to catch them in their mouths.

He nodded at the few people he passed by and was about to enter the men's room when he heard a choking sound coming from the other side of the small building. He thought about ignoring it, but Megan had been gone for close to twenty minutes.

When he walked around the building, he found Megan leaning against it, hunched over, hair hanging down around her face. Her fist was in her mouth, her pale face pulled back into a silent scream.

He didn't touch her. He didn't know her and didn't want to run the risk of comfort being misconstrued for something else. These were strange times. Instead, he mirrored her pose, leaning against the building, leaving a couple of feet between them. He didn't speak, letting her decide how to proceed.

A minute passed, her breath hitching. Another minute. Then another. Then she said, "I hate this." She sniffled, wiping her face with the back of her arm.

Don sighed. "I know. We all do."

He didn't think she heard him. "I'm tired," she said. "Tired of putting on a brave face. Tired of holding this all in because there's nowhere else for it to go. I look at my kids, and I don't know what to do." She looked at him. Don thought she was hanging on by a thread. "How do I tell them? How do I look them in the eye and tell them that they're going to die?"

"I don't know," Don admitted. "Maybe you don't have to. You heard your son. I think he might already know. Or, at least, have some idea."

She took that in, let it simmer. Then, "It's weird. Talking to strangers. It's like therapy, almost. It's easier to tell a stranger something hard than it is to tell someone you love. With strangers, you don't give a shit how they look at you. You'll never see them again."

"I . . . suppose that's one way of thinking of it."

"You're a stranger," she said. "Tell me what to do. Tell me how to make sense of all of this. Tell me how I'm supposed to act, what I'm supposed to say."

Don hesitated. "The truth? Or some version of it. Or maybe you lie to them. Tell them that everything is going to be all right.

One night, you'll all go to bed together and you'll tell stories and eat candy and remind each other that it was all worth it. All of it. Every bit, even when it hurt beyond comprehension. But is that right? Isn't honesty more important?"

She put a hand on her stomach. "I'm pregnant."

"John said as much." Though it was on the tip of his tongue, he managed to catch himself before he added *congratulations*.

"Did he?" she said, absentmindedly rubbing her stomach. "Of course he did. He told everyone when we found out. Only a couple of weeks ago, when everything made sense because the smart people were going to fix everything. We were going to live. It's a girl. I don't know how I know, but I do. I've named her Eleanor. Ellie, for short."

"That's a lovely name," Don said, heart heavy. "Have you told John?"

Suddenly, she raised her hand as if to slap him. Her arm cocked back, her eyes narrowed. She even began to swing her arm. Don flinched—of course he did—but the slap never came. Instead, her arm stopped halfway through the arc. Then her face twisted like she was about to burst into tears, arm falling back to her side.

Don took a step away from her, unsure of what she'd do next.

She snapped, "It's not *for* him. It's mine. It's for me. You'll never understand. How could you? You don't know what it's like. I'm carrying a child inside me, a girl that's barely bigger than a berry. And what am I supposed to do with her? What am I supposed to tell her late at night when I can't sleep? Do I apologize? We put her there. Do I get rid of her? What would be the point?" She bent over once more, hugging herself and coughing. "I'm sorry," she spat out. "I'm sorry, I'm sorry, I'm sorry."

They came back together, Don and Megan. He thought her broken, broken in ways that her husband did not see. She smiled—a lovely, genuine smile not made of plastic—when her children shouted for her, running up and hanging on to her legs. She ran a finger through their hair and exclaimed along with them about the stick they had found, a stick that looked like a sword. When they asked why her makeup was running, if she'd been crying, she laughed and said, "Just thinking some Mommy thoughts. Everything is wonderful now."

Rodney and John stood near the table, a few feet apart. Rodney had that look on his face, the one that said he was about done with people for the day. John's hands were in his hair.

"Thank you for joining us for a meal," Rodney said. "It's time for us to get back on the road."

"Are you sure?" John asked, dropping his hands. He smiled again. Don had never seen anything quite like it. He thought that if he wanted, he could count all of John's teeth. "Minnesota. Might be the best place to go."

"No," Megan said, her children still clutching her legs. "I don't want them to come with us."

"Honey, I think—"

"I will scream," she told him pleasantly. "I will scream and scream until someone comes over and I will tell them that these men tried to hurt us. They need to leave. I don't want them near my children."

Her kids looked up at her with widened eyes.

John looked at Don, a line forming on his forehead. "Did you touch my wife?"

"Okay," Rodney said firmly. "That's enough. No one did anything to anyone. We'll be on our way."

"Did he touch you?" John demanded. "Did he hurt you? Did he hurt the baby?"

"Children!" Megan cried. "First one back to the car gets to pick the song on the radio!" Without looking back, she pushed her children toward the parking lot. Jamie and Lauren protested, but she was stronger than they were.

"I didn't do anything to her," Don said. "She's upset because of— She's upset."

John laughed, a bright and broken sound. "I know. Really, really upset. Did I tell you what I do for a living?"

"No," Rodney said. "You didn't. But that's all right. We'll just—"

"I'm a veterinarian. Love dogs and cats and birds and reptiles. It's hard, though. Animals die. People coming in with tears in their eyes because their pet is acting weird. Sometimes, things turn out all right. Other times, though. Other times, you have to do the right thing, the *kind* thing. Veterinarians have some of the highest suicide rates out of any profession. Did you know that? Vets and vets: veterans and veterinarians. Same boat." He looked back at the van. Megan was turned around in the passenger seat, saying something to the kids. "Phenobarbital. No pain, you just . . . go right to sleep. I brought some. Enough. Just in case."

Rodney took a step back, pulling Don with him. "Why do you need it, John?"

He looked at them, but Don thought he was staring right through them both. "I . . . don't know. A contingency plan? But I have this thought in my head. If it happens, if the fire comes, I don't want to burn. I don't want them to burn. It will hurt. A parent should never let their child feel something like that. And then I ask myself, what would a real man do? A real man wouldn't let bad things happen. A real man would get in front of the problem. A *real* man does the things no one else will do. He'd make it so it doesn't hurt anymore." John began to walk toward the parking lot. He didn't seem to notice he was leaving some of their things behind. A picnic basket. Cups. Uneaten food. He stopped in the grass and looked back over his shoulder at them.

"I'm willing to do whatever I need to."

And then he walked away. To the van. To his awaiting family. He climbed inside. Looked in the back seat to say something to the kids. Then he leaned over and kissed Megan on the cheek. She didn't acknowledge it, staring straight ahead.

The van started up. A moment later, the rear lights flashed white as it backed up. The last they saw of the family was the children pressed against the rear window, waving at them.

Don and Rodney waved back, out of habit.

Then they packed up the remains of the lunch and got back on the road.

That night, while parked on a dirt road surrounded by fields, Don listened as Rodney snored next to him. A familiar sound, comforting. He knew it well. Had gotten used to it too, though sometimes, when Rodney was congested, he slept in the spare bedroom to let Don get a good night's sleep. He was like that. Not to most people, but to Don. Ever since they first met. Over the years, they'd known people who were put off by Rodney. They thought him quiet, too quiet, as if not saying anything was a mark against his character. It wasn't. Rodney just spoke when he had something to say. No more, no less.

The mattress was uncomfortable, but they'd slept on worse. Once, about a year into their relationship—the newness still there, crackling, exciting—Rodney had taken Don camping up in White Mountain National Forest. And not just the normal type of camping with allotted spaces and facilities within walking distance. Wild camping, Rodney had called it. Legal in parts of Maine. You parked your car and went out into the woods. Rules had to be followed, very strict rules, but Rodney was experienced.

They'd camped under an overhanging rock ledge. Two nights. On the second night, a fierce storm had blown in while they were out hiking. Wind blowing the rain sideways, trees bending and swaying. Don had worried they'd gotten lost, but Rodney said they hadn't. He knew where they were, knew where they were going. And twenty minutes later, they'd found their camp, right where Rodney said it was.

Soaked to the bone, they'd dried off in the tent, and one thing led to another, Rodney's hands callused, warm, gentle. At the climax, Don cried out and the sound of his voice echoed through the trees.

Rodney had fallen to the side, Don grimacing at the wetness around his rear. Handing him a towel, Rodney had said, "I think I love you." It was the first time he'd said it out loud.

To that, Don had replied, "I think you do too."

They'd slept tangled together, the rain lashing against the tent.

And here, now, over four decades later, the man snored worse than ever.

Don smiled quietly to himself. The smile faded when he thought of Megan. Of John. Jamie and Lauren, none the wiser. Should he have done more? Said more?

He thought of the small box stored away, and the reunion they were hoping for. Out of sight, but never out of mind. That wasn't possible.

Eventually, he slept.

CHAPTER 3

Uranus was gone. That's what they heard when they turned on the radio on the sixth day of their trip. In a trembling voice, the newscaster said that Uranus had been ripped apart. Given the position of the planets, Jupiter was next. The Great Red Spot—the stormy eye of the planet that had raged on for centuries—didn't hold a candle to what was coming for it.

Don turned the dial on the radio away from the news, right as they began to theorize how electronics would be affected soon: At some point in the coming weeks—perhaps days—satellites would become useless. Internet not working. Cell phones not working. It was necessary information, but at the same time, too much to listen to. Though Rodney would never admit it, Don knew it was making him anxious. He felt the same, responding to texts from friends back home, asking about their journey, how far they'd made it, if they thought they'd have enough time. Too much, all of it. Especially when he'd spent the morning screenshotting the maps on his phone just in case service went down. He found classical music—"Clair de Lune," the bittersweet piano. Then country—Garth Brooks and the thunder rolled. He stopped on Pat Benatar for just a moment as she sang that whatever we deny or embrace for worse or for better, we belong, we belong, we belong together. Back to "Clair de Lune," and there it stayed. Such a terribly sad song. The window down, the air cool, sky cloudy.

It was slow going. They'd just gotten out of New York state, having had to make several detours to avoid major cities and highways. They'd come across long lines of cars, people standing on the road, conversing. They'd met up with a group of young people who'd shown them a way around using dirt roads so small that trees scraped against the side of the RV. They'd almost made it out before they'd gotten stuck in a muddy patch of ground deeper than it looked. The kids had stopped, gotten out, and proceeded to push the RV. By the time it was free, their new friends were covered in mud. They hugged before going their separate ways.

They didn't travel at night. Rodney liked to drive, but his vision wasn't as good as it used to be, and Don didn't trust himself to drive on strange roads in the dark. Thankfully, they chased the sun as they traveled west. They took breaks often, getting out of the RV and stretching, Don massaging Rodney's neck and shoulders as they grew stiff. His back was bothering him too, but he didn't complain much.

On the eighth day since they had started their trip—and with approximately three weeks remaining until the end—they found themselves in rural Ohio. Don had never been to Ohio before. It was flat. So much of it was flat. Large empty fields that stretched on as far as the eye could see, dotted sparsely with withered trees.

It was getting dark, and the two-lane road they were on seemed to grow smaller the farther they went. According to the GPS on Don's phone, they still had another three hours to go before they found a larger road.

No places to pull off. No rest stops, no empty parking lots. Just miles and miles of nothing with darkened houses every now and then. They were about to start arguing—Don could feel it building—when they crested a rare hill and saw a large fire in the distance. Behind it, the sun approaching the horizon.

"What's that?" Don asked nervously. "Is it a house? Do we try and call the fire department?" In his mind, he could imagine the fields catching on fire, surrounding them, keeping them from finishing what they'd started out to do.

"Too small," Rodney said. "See sunlight flashing near it? Cars. I think it's a bonfire."

He was right. As they got closer, they could see people standing around the large fire. It looked to be in the middle of a field, surrounded by at least a dozen vehicles: cars, SUVs, campers. Tents too, some small for only one or two people, and others much larger that could easily fit at least five adults with room to spare.

They stopped on the blacktop as they came to a dirt road that led up to the bonfire. No one behind them. No one in front of them.

"Well?" Don asked. "What are we doing?"

"Hush," Rodney said, staring straight ahead. "I'm thinking."

They both let out yelps when a knock came at the passenger window.

Don jerked away from the door, only to have his seat belt pull tight against his chest. He pressed a hand against his throat as he turned his head.

A young woman stood outside the RV. She looked to be in her early twenties, and was stunningly beautiful. Her long, cascading hair rested on her shoulders. Atop her head, a crown of white daisies with yellow centers. She wore a cropped shirt, her bare stomach pale, and a long flowing pink skirt with lace. She was barefoot, her toenails painted lime green.

Don cracked the window.

The woman stepped closer. She smiled. "Hi. Are you lost?"

"I don't . . . think so?" Don said. "We're headed west."

"Where?"

"Washington state."

Her eyes widened. "That's far away."

"I know."

She said, "You're headed west, but the road you're coming up on can get a little tricky. It's better during the day." She glanced back over her shoulder. Don could hear music now, coming from the people around the fire. Bob Marley and the Wailers. They shot the sheriff, but they didn't shoot no deputy. People danced, hands high above their heads. Turning back to them, the woman said, "You wouldn't hurt anyone, would you? Rob someone. Take something that doesn't belong to you."

Don shook his head slowly. "I don't think we'd know how."

The woman chuckled. "You can stay with us for tonight, if you want. We have wine and weed and the vibes are to die for. We also have chili, if you're hungry. One of the people in the caravan used to be a chef and had some venison."

"Used to be?" Don asked.

The woman leaned forward, her face inches from the window. "Well, we *all* used to be something, didn't we? Now, we're something else. Room to park. We'll see you up there?" And with that, she spun on her bare heels and walked back toward the fire, her skirt billowing around her feet.

"What do you think?" Don asked, staring after the woman.

"Hippies," Rodney muttered. "It's always gotta be hippies. You hear her? She said they have a commune."

"Caravan," Don corrected without thinking.

Rodney waved a hand. "Same difference. Caravan leads to communes which leads to Communism."

"Rodney."

"What?"

"I don't think that matters anymore."

Rodney opened his mouth to retort, but no sound came out. He tried again. Nothing. He sighed. "It matters to *me*."

"Duly noted. I'm tired. And hungry. Let's go hang out with the hippies and their wine and weed."

Rodney gaped at him.

Don stared back.

Grumbling, Rodney put the RV in drive and pulled down the road.

The woman was waiting for them. She clapped when they parked and turned off the RV, hurrying to the passenger door to fling it open. In her hand, another flower crown. She curtsied neatly in front of Don as he clambered out of the RV. Then she placed the flower crown on his head before kissing the tip of his nose. "There," she said, taking a step back. "Now you look the part." Dropping her voice, she whispered, "I don't think your travel companion wants one."

"He's my husband," Don said. "And no, I don't think you should try and give him one."

Rodney rounded the RV and rolled his eyes when he saw Don's new accessory. "I'll leave you here," he threatened.

"You wouldn't dare," Don said.

Rodney demurred, grimacing as he glared at the flower crown.

"My name is Pantomime," the woman said. "What are yours?"

Rodney groaned. "Are you out of your—"

"I'm Don," he said quickly. "This is Rodney. It's a pleasure to meet you . . . Pantomime."

She grinned at them. "Oh, aren't you precious. Come on, let me introduce you to my friends."

And she did just that. They met everyone, people with names like Corn Blue and Violetta and Aberdeen. They were all young, the oldest appearing around thirty, or thereabouts. There was food and fire smoke and weed smoke. Plastic cups filled with white wine, with red wine. Stacks of wood for the fire. Speakers set up on the back of a truck, the music blaring. The biggest bong Don had ever seen, at least five feet tall and popular, if the line was any indication.

Don and Rodney took a seat on a log about ten feet from the bonfire, the flames rising and crackling toward the sky. And that was to say nothing of the sky itself: stars in only half the sky. The other half was pure black, as if those stars had all been swallowed up. Or, that something was so close that it blocked the light from ever reaching them.

Pantomime had disappeared after making sure they were settled in, reappearing a few minutes later carrying two bowls filled with chili. She gave them each a bowl and pulled two plastic spoons out of a pocket on her skirt. Rodney made a face as he took the spoon from her, but otherwise didn't react.

She sat down next to them, stretching her long legs out toward the fire. Her toes dug into the coarse grass of the field. Across from them, people sat or stood in small groups, laughing and chatting away. On the other side of the fire, two women slow danced, their heads on each other's shoulders.

"So," Pantomime said as Don and Rodney dug into their food. "How's it going?"

Don stopped, his spoon halfway to his mouth. "It's . . . going?"

She nodded as if that was the answer she expected. "That's fair. And probably as best an answer as any of us can hope for."

Rodney snorted into his chili. Pantomime either didn't hear him or ignored him.

"We're going to Canada," she said. "Came up from Houston." She shook her head. "Had to get out of the city while we still could.

Military were in the streets, telling everyone to stay at home, to stay off the roads." She looked at them with eyes reflecting the firelight. "A lot of people refused, so they were shot and killed."

"Jesus Christ," Don muttered.

"It's happening all over," she said. "I don't know why anyone expected anything different. You tell people that nothing can save them, and what do you think is going to happen? For them to just lie there and take it? For them to say, oh, well, we had a good run? That's not how humans work."

"And how do they work?" Rodney asked, his tone sardonic.

Pantomime laughed. "We're animals. All of us. Take away the sense of societal normalcy, and everyone turns at least a little bit feral."

"Did you?" Don asked.

"Can't turn into something I already was." She shrugged. "I've accepted who and what I am. It took me a long time, and now, with everything . . . I might as well be the real me while I still have the chance."

"Why does it take the end of the world to be you?" Rodney asked.

"Why are you going to Washington now?" she countered, neat as you please. "Why not last month, last year?"

Rodney glared down at his chili.

"Did I upset him?" she whispered in Don's ear.

"Yes," Don said. "But he's always a little upset."

Pantomime laughed. "Aren't we all? It's strange, really. How different we all are. And yet, it's universal. Things like anger. Grief. Happiness. Maybe the causes aren't quite the same, but we all know what it feels like to laugh. To cry. To rage. Have you accepted the truth?" She plucked at the flower crown on Don's head.

"What truth?" he asked.

"That we're all in this moment together. We're all going the same way. It doesn't matter what color you are. Your background. Your beliefs. Your heritage. Who you love. Everyone, right now, is all the same. There's something beautiful about that."

"So," Rodney said, "those people who were shot. Those people who died. That's beautiful?"

"Of course not," Pantomime said. She didn't seem offended. "That's horror. That's ugly. But then that's also humanity, isn't it? Look at us, in the middle of nowhere. We're celebrating the fact that we're here. Right now, in this moment, we're alive. Some would want to take that from us without a second thought. Because they're following orders or because they have malice in their hearts and the permission to act on it. It's the duality of humanity. One side, capable of great love, the other, great harm. There's nothing like us anywhere." She perked up when a new song—the B-52s and "Love Shack"—began to spill from the speakers. "I'll be right back. Don't go anywhere!" She stood and practically floated toward the fire. A man wrapped his arms around her shoulders as they both started to sing at the top of their lungs.

"What have you gotten us into?" Rodney asked.

"I notice you finished all the food they provided."

"It wasn't bad," Rodney muttered. "Not spicy enough."

"Yes, I'm sure we can let the chef know. I bet he'll comp the meal."

"Please do. And no corn bread? I want to speak to the manager. You *must* have corn bread with chili."

"I'll get right on that."

Rodney said, "Hey."

Don looked upon his worn and lovely face. "Hey."

"You ever think we'd end up in a field in Ohio with hippies?"

"I'm surprised it hadn't happened to us before, to be quite honest."

"Sass," Rodney said fondly. "Always with the sass."

Pantomime brought the man over. They'd met him briefly before but hadn't caught his name. He introduced himself as Juniper, and Rodney looked as if he wanted to jump into the fire.

"Pantomime said you're married?" Juniper asked as he sat on the log with them, Pantomime in his lap, her long legs dangling off his. The man had long, beautiful hair that was braided and hanging off his shoulder. In the braid, wildflowers and twigs.

"We are," Don said.

"For how long?"

"Legally, since 2015. But much longer than that."

"Forty years," Rodney said.

"Holy shit," Juniper whispered. "That's longer than any of us have been alive."

"Yes, well," Don said, used to the fact that most young people viewed older folks as dusty exhibits in a museum.

Juniper laughed. "I like you. You're funny. Me and Pantomime, we want to get married. Haven't been together near as long as you two, but when you know, you know."

"And how long have you been an item?" Don asked.

Juniper frowned, the lines on his forehead deep. "Uh . . . hold on. Three—no, *four* months."

"Four months," Pantomime agreed. "The best four months I've ever had."

"Oh my god," Rodney said.

"Yes," Don said quickly. "That's exactly right. Oh my god, how wonderful."

"I saw her at a farmers market. Selling these wicked hemp bags. I must have bought three of them before I got the nerve to ask her out."

"He was so awkward," Pantomime said, smacking a kiss on the top of his head. "I thought he was trying to case the joint so he could rob me later."

"At a farmers market," Rodney said dryly.

"Exactly," Pantomime said. "Luckily for me, he wasn't planning on armed robbery. He was after something else."

"Her heart," Juniper said seriously.

"That's achingly romantic," Don said. He didn't like to lie, but sometimes, a situation called for it. This seemed like one of them. "Congratulations."

They both beamed. "Thank you," Juniper said. "We all float through space on a rock, hurtling toward forever. So many of us forget that it's other people who make life worth living. As much as we like to think so, we can't do this alone. Everyone needs someone. Maybe not all the time, but enough that it matters. And hey, you could give us some advice. How have you made it work?"

"Made what work?" Rodney asked.

"The two of you," Pantomime said.

Rodney and Don looked at each other. Rodney shook his head pointedly. Don ignored him. "I suppose it's different for everyone. You could say it all comes down to love, but is that really all there is?" He paused. Then, "That's a big part of it, perhaps the biggest, but I also respect him. I trust him. I know he wants what's best for me, even if that means telling me something I don't want to hear."

We have to live, Rodney whispered in his head, a memory, desperate and aching. *It's not fair what happened—I want to scream until I can't anymore—but we're still here.*

Rodney touched the back of his hand.

"That's lovely," Pantomime said. "Why are you going to Washington?"

They both froze. Don shouldn't have said where they were going. A mistake, a slip of the tongue. Don couldn't get the words out.

Rodney said, "Something we need to see to."

She didn't push. "I hope it's everything you've been looking for."

Don bristled, a bright burst of anger, unbidden. Or was it? Guilt did that to a person, didn't it? "We're not looking for anything. We know what we're going to find."

Rodney dropped his hand on top of Don's. Not as a warning, but to let Don know he was there.

"Okay," Pantomime said easily, as if they were discussing the weather. "Whatever it is, you'll succeed. I feel it."

Don deflated. "I'm sorry. I shouldn't have snapped."

Juniper laughed. "That was you snapping? My guy, you're allowed. Hell, we all are. What's the point of knowing the end is coming if you can't scream and wail about it? I have. Does it help? I don't know. But I know how I feel when I finish."

"Better," Pantomime said.

"Much better," Juniper agreed. "We got this energy in us, right? Sometimes, it needs to be released before it consumes us. We're like black holes, in a way. Sucking in all the light and stardust until it has nowhere else to go but out."

"That's not how black holes work," Rodney grumbled.

"Would you like a cookie?" Pantomime asked. "They have THC, but it's not too strong. I've had a couple, and I'm feeling pretty great." She lifted her legs, flexing her toes. "Better than great, even. I like being alive."

"I'm glad you do," Juniper said, his face in her hair. He turned his head slightly to look at Don and Rodney. "What do you think happens next?"

Rodney and Don exchanged glances. Rodney asked, "Next?"

"After we die," Juniper said. "When the black hole eats the Earth, where do we go?"

Hadn't they talked about this? For hours and hours and hours. Not because of the black hole, not because the world was ending. No, this came before, when things were somehow worse. Rodney went in circles, one moment believing in the idea of Heaven, the next, saying there was nothing, that it was all empty space where everything was black.

Don didn't agree, not quite. He wasn't sure about the idea of Heaven—it sounded like an exclusive club that could turn away anyone for any reason. Granted, the alternative—if one believed such things—was downstairs where it got a little hot. But if the religious version of what came next was wrong, what did that mean? Where would they go? And *what* would go? The soul—who even knew what that was. Perhaps it was the mind, the consciousness. Would the body be there?

Don said, "I don't know."

Juniper shrugged. "That's fair. I think it's all about energy. Each of us has this energy, coded deep within us, something from the universe, like a little fire being lit. Some burn brighter than others, but that's the way of things. And when it's our time to go, our energy returns to where it came from. Little streaks of light, like a comet." He chuckled. "Can you imagine what it's going to be like when all of us go at the same time? That much energy released into the universe? Man, I'd love to see that. I bet it's going to be brighter than the sun."

"Why?" Don asked. "Why do you think that?"

Pantomime smiled. "Because we're scared."

Pantomime brought them weed cookies. One each, with strict instructions to eat half and then wait to see how they felt before deciding if they wanted the other half. Peanut butter, little fork marks across the top. They looked significantly more edible than the muffins they'd been given before they departed.

"When was the last time we got stoned?" Don asked Rodney as the Bee Gees began singing about stayin' alive.

Rodney turned the cookie over in his hands. "Not since the nineties."

Don nodded. And then, without thinking too much about it, broke the cookie in half and shoved it in his mouth. He chewed furiously, swallowing it down as best he could before he changed his mind.

Rodney sighed.

Don set the other half of the cookie on his lap. "Well, then. That's that."

"Last time we smoked," Rodney said, "you thought the Queen of England was coming over. That apartment we had, remember? The one with the hot water that never worked. You spent almost an hour being mad we didn't have any tea. You said that we were probably going to be executed."

Don sniffed. "I don't remember that at all. And it wasn't tea, it was tea *cakes*. There's a difference."

Rodney said, "Yeah, yeah." And then he split his cookie and ate half. He didn't look at Don as he chewed, gaze firmly fixed on the fire. "Probably all stems and seeds. Won't even feel anything."

An hour later, Rodney had a flower crown of his very own. Someone had also given him a pair of fairy wings, strapped to his back like a backpack. They were sparkly and pink and he didn't seem to mind them very much, even if he'd threatened the first three people who'd tried to put them on him. Don laughed, feeling floaty, feeling *fine*. He loved the way the grass felt against his hands, the soft give of the earth.

The fire stayed large and hot, sparks rising toward the blackened sky. People danced, people sang, people painted each other with greens and blues and reds. One woman—a tiny little thing, kissing five feet, but barely—walked across burning coals, her face a tight mask of concentration.

Pantomime sat next to Don, her arm through his. They watched as Juniper tried to convince Rodney that a little body paint never hurt anyone. Rodney did not seem to agree.

"You love him," Pantomime said to Don, her head on his shoulder.

"I do."

"Why?"

"Because I choose to," Don said. "He's funny. And sarcastic. Keeps me in check. Never once has he said a dream of mine wasn't possible. Never once has he made me feel like I'm somehow lesser. I've tried to do the same for him because that's what he deserves. At one point, early on in our relationship, I worried that I was holding him back. We weren't out, not really, and I thought maybe he'd be better off without me."

"What did he say to that?"

Don smiled quietly. "Said I needed to get those foolish thoughts out of my head because he was in this for the long haul. I believed him. I believed *in* him. Still do, in fact. Now more than ever."

"Do you have any regrets?"

"Hundreds. Thousands. When you get to be as old as we are, you rack them up like a collection of gaudy knickknacks."

"I'm scared," she admitted. "I try not to be, but I am. Not of dying. I've made peace with that. But how will I act in the moments just before? Will I cry? Will I beg for more time? Will I pray to a god I don't believe in on the chance that there's something else, something more? I'm not scared of the end, but of what it's going to be like just before it comes."

"You said it yourself. Right now, we're all the same. Everyone is thinking some variation of what you are."

"Do you think there will be music? Wherever we go when we're gone, do you think we'll still be able to sing?"

"I hope so," Don said.

"Remember the *Voyager*?"

Don nodded. "The satellite sent to space. The one with the gold record."

"Actually, it was a space probe," Pantomime said. "A lot of people don't know there are two versions of *Voyager*, the first and the second, and both held the gold record. Do you know who made them? Carl Sagan and Timothy Ferris. On the records, they put photographs of the Earth, of the life-forms on it. Size comparisons of humans to animals. Pictures of men in competition, pictures of gridlocked traffic, pictures of buildings, of mountains, of trees. A South Asian woman breastfeeding. A Black woman looking through a microscope. Thatched huts. People with spears. Drawings of animals. Math equations. Pictures of astronauts, of the moon. But you know what my favorite part is?"

Don shook his head.

"The sounds they included. Music from all over the world. 'Tsuru no Sugomori' from Japan. Bach performed by a German orchestra. Chuck Berry with 'Johnny B. Goode.' Stravinsky. Louis Armstrong. Beethoven. A Navajo night chant. And the noise of Earth, too. Volcanoes and earthquakes. Wind. Rain. The crashing of ocean waves. The sounds of footsteps, of laughter, of a heartbeat. And the *languages*. They had people from all over the world record greetings. In Burmese, in English, in Korean, in Polish, in Urdu. It was all pretty simple, an economy to the language. 'Peace and happiness to all' or 'We wish you everything good from our planet' or, my favorite: 'Greetings from a computer programmer in the little university town of Ithaca on planet Earth.' That one was in Swedish." She looked away. "I think about that a lot."

"Why?" Don asked.

Pantomime shrugged. "If either of the Voyager probes escaped the pull of the black hole, then they're still out there, somewhere. Maybe one day, they'll be discovered. Maybe our voices will be heard again, even though we're no longer here. And what a legacy that is. Coming together to make something so impossible, something so *human*, and then sending it to the stars. We filled it with so much of what makes us tick that it's overwhelming. But isn't it a lie? Say that the records are found. They're listened to. We're heard, even though there's no one left to confirm. What will those beings think? That we were loving, kind, and hopeful? Is that what we deserve?"

Funnily enough, it was Rodney's idea. With bloodshot eyes and a goofy grin, he brought Juniper and Pantomime back to Don, holding both of their hands. Rodney still wore the wings. The other half of his cookie was gone. He'd eaten it.

Which explained why he said, "I'm going to marry Juniper and Pantomime."

Don—ever the voice of reason—said, "Congratulations, but I'm pretty sure we're married, and that constitutes bigamy. Which is illegal."

Rodney grimaced, pulling his hands away from Juniper and Pantomime. "That's not what I meant. I *meant* that *I'm* going to marry *them*."

"Funny, that sounded like you just repeated the same thing."

"Officiate!" Rodney shouted.

"Oh. Well, I suppose that makes more sense. Except for the fact that you're not qualified to do that."

"It's okay," Pantomime said. "It's not like laws matter anymore."

Don frowned. "Yes . . . well . . . huh."

Rodney crossed his arms. "If we don't do this in the next minute, I'm going to change my mind and go to bed."

Juniper looked at Don with pleading eyes. "Please, man. This is, like, everything I have ever wanted. You can come too."

"Thank you," Don said. "I was waiting for my invitation."

Rodney scowled at him. "You're high."

"So are you."

Rodney giggled.

Don did too.

With the moon high above them, Rodney said, "Uh, okay. Hold on. Let me think. All right. We are gathered here tonight with hippies who don't have real names. Two of them want to get married. That's fine with me. But I'm only marrying these two, so the rest of you, stop asking."

Everyone looked on at Juniper and Pantomime standing before each other, hands clasped between them. A red ribbon had been tied around each of their wrists, binding them together.

Rodney continued, adjusting his flower crown. "These are strange times. Nothing makes sense. I'm in Ohio, and I don't know why. I don't like Ohio. I don't like hippies, and here I am, talking to a bunch of them. Strange times, indeed. But these two people want to get married, and that's the only thing that matters. Juniper, do you love Pantomime?"

"Yes," he said.

"And Pantomime, do you love Juniper?"

"Yes, yes," she said, eyes wet.

"Then by the power vested in—what am I talking about? I don't have any power." He paused, lines forming on his forehead. "I'm . . . powerless," he said. He looked at Don. "There was nothing we could've done to stop it."

Don breathed in. Don breathed out.

"I feel lost, sometimes," Rodney said. "But then I see Don. I see his face. I hear his voice. I've known it—him—for decades. The best of times, the worst of times. But he's still here, and I know that means something. I know because I choose to believe it, just like I chose to love him." He looked back at Juniper and Pantomime. "You have a choice. You get to choose who you love. No matter what happens next, no one can take that away from you."

There were no rings. Turned out, throwing an impromptu wedding meant certain things weren't included. But Juniper and Pantomime didn't seem to mind. As soon as Rodney announced them as husband and wife, Juniper dipped Pantomime and kissed her sweetly, his braid hanging down the sides of their faces. The crowd around them howled their joy to the sky.

They danced, that night. All of them. They danced into the early hours of the morning. Rodney too, though he refused the hand of anyone who asked. Aside from Don, that is. They moved away from the fire, away from the people. They danced in the shadows of the dark, pressed chest to chest, swaying slightly, feet shuffling through the grass.

"What an odd day," Don said, a little more sober than he'd been during the ceremony.

"We've had odder."

"Have we? I can't remember."

In the distance, near the fire, Juniper and Pantomime were in their own little world, hugging each other close.

Rodney said, "It's not fair."

Many things were unfair. Don didn't know which thing Rodney meant, and said as much.

"They're just kids. They don't get to have what we had. Have."

"A long life," Don whispered.

Rodney nodded. "They don't get to spend weeks and years waking up next to each other. They don't get to see the world together without thinking about how it'll all be gone soon enough. They don't get a chance to just *be*."

"Don't they?" Don asked. "It might not be as long as we've had, but they have it now. I don't think you could have given them a greater gift."

Rodney scowled. "I didn't do anything."

Don kissed the underside of his jaw. "Okay."

They left the caravan early the next morning, the sun barely peeking above the horizon. A heavy mist hung over the field, low curls of fog at their feet. Juniper and Pantomime joined them outside their RV, the pair wrapped in a wool blanket.

"Where will you go?" Don asked them.

Juniper grinned. "Thinking about a honeymoon. The Poconos, in Pennsylvania. Cabins up there. Seems like a good place to sit out the rest of time."

"All of you going?"

Pantomime shrugged. "Maybe. Most are still headed for Canada, but the borders might be an issue. Everything is shut down. No one going in or out. If they try, they'll have to be smart about it. What about you two? Washington, still?"

Don nodded. "Washington."

She cocked her head quizzically. "Will you find what you're looking for there?"

"Yes," Rodney said, and Don believed him.

Rodney and Don took turns hugging Juniper and Pantomime. When Rodney and Juniper came together, Juniper whispered something in Rodney's ear. Rodney didn't move. When Juniper pulled away, Rodney said, "Been doing it for this long. Can't stop now. Won't stop now."

As they drove down the small hill back to the road, a line of people stood next to the remains of the bonfire, waving under the morning sky.

When they were out of sight, Don asked, "What did Juniper say to you?"

Rodney's hands tightened on the steering wheel. "Some hippie bullshit."

"Rodney."

He sighed. "He said that I'm to love you forever."

"And you can't stop?"

"Can't. Won't. Not now, not ever."

They drove on.

After a time, Don reached over and took Rodney's hand in his. It was enough.

CHAPTER 4

Jupiter would fall in the next few days.

They left the radio on, sometimes, to be kept informed. Cities burning. Cities on lockdown. Chaos in Europe, Asia, Canada, in Africa, in South America. In the United States, the president urged calm, peace. Like a stern grandfather, he admonished those who looted, rioted, those who screamed and begged for help. "There's only so much I can tolerate," he said, sounding ancient and worn, no different than he'd been previously. "Consider this a final warning: Anyone caught breaking the law will be dealt with as swiftly and harshly as the situation calls for. Why make the last days so difficult? Let us pray."

After that, Rodney turned the radio dial until he found classical music. Polonaise-Fantaisie by Chopin. He left it there.

Indiana. Illinois. It was slow going. Rodney didn't like to drive more than a few hours at a stretch. They had time, but every now and then, Don would think, *What if it happens sooner? What if we don't make it?*

They saw others on the road. People in cars, in RVs both bigger and smaller than their own. As they crossed Illinois, they were forced onto highways with more and more lanes. The back roads they'd been trying to keep to proved to be too much for the RV. Heavy rain turned some of the roads into muddy swamps, and Rodney didn't want them to get stuck in case no one could help them. Don kept their phones charged, the warnings about loss of service ringing in his ears. He continued to screenshot their route, making sure to include alternatives in case a road or highway was impassable. They had the paper map in the glove box, but at least they'd have backup in case the map was too difficult to read.

They knew they were in trouble when they reached a four-lane blacktop and immediately were forced to slow to a crawl. In front of them, red taillights stretched on as far as the eye could see. They stayed in the far-right lane. To their left, a row of stopped traffic, a concrete divider, and then two lanes in the opposite direction, mostly empty. To their right, trees dotted the landscape, sparse. In the distance, thicker trees.

"Shit," Rodney muttered as he brought the RV to a stop, leaving a car's length of distance between them and the vehicle in front. The radio had long been switched off. "What do you think?"

Don squinted down at his phone. He wasn't very good at using it, but he could find his way around most of it. "The GPS is all messed up. Says the road should be clear."

"Goddamn machines," Rodney said, leaning forward to look out the windshield. "I don't want to be stuck here."

Don looked in the side mirror. A sedan had pulled up behind them, practically kissing their rear bumper. "It looks like we don't have a choice."

Up ahead, people were getting out of their cars, standing on their tiptoes or with their hands on their hips. Some spoke to each other. Others looked panicked.

"Stay here," Rodney said. "I'm going to see what's going on."

"Are you sure that's a good idea?"

"You think of anything else?"

"No."

"Okay," Rodney said, and got out of the RV. He grunted as he stepped down to the pavement. Looking back the way they'd come, he shook his head. Hitching his pants, he marched toward the people gathered a car ahead. Don rolled down the window to hear as best he could. In the distance, the sound of honking horns. It smelled of exhaust and cow manure.

Rodney reached three men and a woman standing next to a blue sedan. He greeted them and asked if they knew what the holdup was, and how long it was going to take.

"Trailer jackknifed a few miles ahead," the woman said. "Blocking both lanes of traffic. Apparently, the cops were called, but that was an hour ago."

"Any other way around?" Rodney asked.

One of the men shook his head. "Not unless you plan on going off-roading. Too many people have gotten stuck and had to abandon their cars."

But whatever else they said was drowned out by the sound of a revving engine. Don turned his head to the left. Next to their RV, a truck. Older model. Half the size of the RV. Inside, Don saw a man behind the wheel. Couldn't see his face, just his thick arms with dark hair. In front of the truck, a white two-door car, empty, the occupants standing on the road.

Don frowned as the man revved the engine again. He was about to call for Rodney when the truck shot forward, smashing into the back of the white car, knocking it askew. Windows shattered, metal crumpled, and Don jerked away, hitting his head against the frame of the door.

The truck reversed, tires squealing, bumper tearing off and landing on the ground. Don watched as Rodney whirled around, eyes wide.

No one ran.

One of the men Rodney had been standing with started screaming, his face splotchy, spittle flying from his mouth. "What the fuck! What the fuck! That's my *car*, you piece of shit! What the hell are you doing?"

The truck roared again as it plowed forward, striking the white car once more, knocking it into the vehicle in front of it. In that car, teenagers, two of them, both staring over the back seat to see what had hit them.

The owner of the white car pulled a gun out from a holster on his side.

Don's throat closed, breath whistling. He couldn't speak, couldn't shout in warning.

"What the fuck!" the man shouted again, pointing the gun at the truck. "What the fuck!"

He fired, the sound a sharp crack.

A moment of silence, as if everyone held their breath. Then:

Now people began to scream. *Now* people began to run. As the bullet struck the grille of the truck with a comical *twang*—like Looney Tunes, Don thought through a haze of panic—the driver of the truck reversed again, much faster, crashing into the vehicle that had come to a stop behind it. The truck's front was crumpled, bent brackets and torn metal twisted into sharp points. The man with the gun fired again. Spiderweb cracks appeared on the windshield of the truck.

Don screamed when the door to the RV flew open. Rodney scrambled inside, staying low. "Get *down*," he snarled at Don, twisting the key to the RV. The engine whined as it clicked over, but Rodney didn't wait for it to settle. Glancing back and forth at the side mirrors, he quickly reversed, the RV shuddering. They smashed into the car behind them, Rodney and Don jerking in their seats.

"Oh my god," Don whispered as another shot was fired, then another. "Oh my god."

"Hold on," Rodney said, putting the RV in drive and twisting the wheel to the right. They shot forward, hitting the ditch on the side of the road, both bouncing in their seats. "Seat belt, now!"

Don belted in. Behind them, screams. In the side mirror, Don could see people running down the road or huddled behind their cars. The gunman approached the passenger side of the truck. He raised the gun. He fired, the window shattering. And then he fired again.

The American Dream, Don thought as tree limbs scraped against the sides of the RV. *Death by gunfire.*

The RV bounced up and down, the seat belt pulling painfully against Don's chest. The ground seemed to be holding, not like the swamps they'd had to avoid. He didn't say a word, not wanting Rodney's concentration to be broken.

It was almost fifteen minutes later when they came onto a dirt road. The RV made it onto the road, and Rodney came to a stop, panting, head pressed against the steering wheel.

"What happened?" Don whispered.

Rodney jerked his head up. Hands reaching in a panic, he said, "Did you get hit? Are you hurt? Tell me now!" He rubbed Don's arms, his shoulders, his chest, stomach. Took Don's hands in his and inspected them, turning them over. When he saw Don wasn't injured, he sat back in his seat and exhaled loudly. "Jesus Christ."

"What happened?"

Rodney shook his head. "I don't know. One minute, I was talking to those people, and the next, I was driving away. I don't even remember getting back into the RV."

"I'm calling the police. Someone could be hurt." He began to dial 911, but Rodney placed his hand over the screen. "What are you doing?"

"Police won't help," Rodney said grimly. "You heard them. No one came to the accident. And remember what Pantomime said? They're killing people, Don."

He dropped the phone in his lap. "What do we do now?"

"We continue on."

"But what about—"

"There's nothing we can do. If you think I'm going to drive you back toward the gun, you're mistaken."

"I saw teenagers."

Rodney swallowed thickly. "I know."

They didn't speak much after that, especially when they found a bullet hole in the rear of the RV, right above the bumper. Don had noticed it after getting out to make sure the tires were still intact. Rodney stared at the hole for a long time before shaking his head.

Nothing was damaged inside, as far as they could tell. Some things had fallen during their escape, but nothing was broken, nothing ruined. The box was safely stored away. Don breathed a sigh of relief; he didn't want to return it damaged. They never found where the bullet went.

They were in luck: The road they were on ran mostly parallel with the freeway, though was far enough away that they couldn't be seen. They would have to take it slow, but no one else seemed to know it existed. It wasn't on any of Don's screenshots. No houses, no mailboxes. No other signs of life aside from a wooden fence that had long ago fallen into disrepair. He wondered about the people on the main road. If he and Rodney should have done more. If they should have been braver. Or more foolish? Was there a difference? Don didn't know.

Rodney was hunched over the steering wheel, the corners of his lips tugging down. Don didn't push, knowing Rodney was working toward something. Don could see it in the set of his shoulders, the way the muscles in his jaw twitched.

About ten minutes later, he stopped the RV, and put it in park. And then he sat back in his chair, breathing in, breathing out.

Don waited.

Rodney said, "I know what you're thinking."

"Tell me."

"We should have done more."

Don looked out the window.

"I know you think that. And maybe I do too. But now is the time to do what *we're* supposed to do. Nothing else can get in the way of that."

"I know," Don said quietly.

"We promised. We have to show up for him."

"I know that too."

They sat in silence for a time.

Rodney said, "I wish . . ." He laughed, a low, bitter thing. "I wish things never had to be this way. I wish we were at home. I wish we were at home, and I can hear you singing in the garden through an open window. I'm inside—"

"—sitting on the recliner."

"Sitting on the recliner, yes, fine. And it's wonderful. It's wonderful because we know what's expected of us. But here . . . out here, I don't know." He sighed as he slumped in his seat. "We might not even make it. It was just an estimate of how long we have left. Maybe it'll end today. Tomorrow."

"We have to try," Don said. "I couldn't stand it if we didn't."

"I know," Rodney said. "Doesn't make it easier."

"Nothing about him has ever been easy."

Rodney looked at him. Don stared back. Rodney smiled quietly. Don nodded.

They moved on.

Before they came across the girl lying in the middle of the road, they hadn't seen much of anyone. Making their way through Iowa, they'd marveled at how flat everything was, how linear. No hills or mountains interrupted the landscape. Halfway through Iowa, a fierce storm blew in, winds whipping the spring blooms on flowers and trees. The rain fell in sheets, sideways, the sky a mass of gray-and-black clouds, thunder rumbling loudly, lightning tearing through the sky. Some houses with lights on, some houses darkened as if no one had lived there for years. Cars, but not many. Once, they went a full hour without seeing any other vehicle.

But now a storm came in, rocking the RV side to side. They parked at an abandoned gas station, the windows cracked, the letters on the sign above the building reading: ICE LOTTO GAS REPENT WHILE YOU STILL CAN. GOD'S GRACE IS INFINITE.

They sat in the RV, pot bubbling on the small stove. Canned stew. Slightly stale bread. The last of their apples for dessert. And it was while Rodney was cutting the apples that Don said, "Don't you think it's funny?"

Rodney grunted without looking up at him, flicking out the apple seeds with the tip of his knife. He handed over a slice, and Don bit into it, the snap crisp.

"It's funny," Don said as he chewed. "This is probably going to be the last time I have an apple."

The hand holding the knife trembled slightly.

"I like apples," Don continued. "Red ones. Green ones. Pink ones. I read once they can make a single tree that has many different types of apples. Who did that? Why did they do it? I don't know. But I like apples. I like the way they taste. The texture. And then I start thinking of everything I've never gotten to try."

"Like what?"

Don thought for a moment. "Snails."

Rodney grimaced. "Out of everything, you pick *snails*?"

Don shrugged as he bit into another slice of apple. The wind moaned around the RV. "Some people like it. Maybe I would have too. You?"

"Ice cream."

"You've had ice cream. Lots of it. More than you should."

"But I haven't had every kind," Rodney said.

"Apple ice cream."

"Snail ice cream."

They laughed.

Rain splashed against the windshield. Thunder loud. Lightning bright.

"Where do you wish we'd visited?" Don asked.

Rodney said, "Italy. I always thought we'd make it. Eating the food. Drinking wine. Looking at old buildings."

"In the countryside, a handsome man as our tour guide."

"He'd flirt with you and I'd have to put him in his place."

"You would, wouldn't you? Giacomo, his name would be Giacomo."

Rodney nodded. "Knock him to the floor."

"My hero."

"Tell him I may look like I'm old, but I can handle my own."

"I'd tell you to stop being so ridiculous, that I could *never* be with anyone else."

"And he'd cry and wail and beg, but you love me too much."

"Unless he has a scooter," Don said. "If he has a little pink Vespa, it's over between us."

"Duly noted. If that's the case, he can have you."

"I don't want to miss things," Don said. "But I can feel it already, like an infection working its way through me. Apples. *Apples.* How stupid is that? I never gave apples a real thought in my life. And now, all I can do is wonder why I didn't. All I can do is think about apples. What else have I missed? What else was right in front of me this entire time but I just . . . ignored it? Ignored it because I assumed it was always going to be there, no matter what. But they're not because there won't be anything left. If it was just humans going, I could accept that. I really think I could. It's always felt like we were living on borrowed time. Not as individuals, but as a species. If it was just humans, and the plants and animals were to live, I think . . . I think I'd find peace in that. Knowing that one day, far, far from now, something will find an apple on a tree and eat it." He sucked in a shaking breath, eyes burning. "But it's not that. It's everything. No more apples."

Rodney wrapped a hand around his shoulders, pulling him close. Don shook as tears leaked from his eyes. "Yes," Rodney said into Don's hair. "But at least I won't have to watch you eat snails."

Don choked on a laugh as he felt Rodney grin. He pulled back slightly, turning up his face. Rodney kissed his cheeks, his chin, the tip of his nose.

"We'll sleep here tonight," Rodney said as they looked out the window into the rain.

"In a little while," Don said. "Let's just . . . sit here, for a bit."

And so they did.

If they'd gone north from Iowa, they'd have entered Minnesota. They decided against it. Odds were firmly against them running into that family again, the ones who'd said they were going to try to survive in Minnesota. Don could still picture John's and Megan's smiles, twisted up into a rictus. She was pregnant, she'd said. John was thinking of ending things, he'd said.

So no, they didn't go north. They continued west, crossing from Iowa into South Dakota. Fewer people here, though Don wasn't surprised. South Dakota was a wide state that barely had anyone living in it. Vast expanses of open land as far as the eye could see. Mountains again, finally. Trees, too, so many trees. A river wound its way alongside them for hours before disappearing into the foothills.

They managed to find an open service station. A few cars in the parking lot, men drinking inside. Not quite drunk, but on their way. They wanted to talk. They wanted to ask if Rodney and Don had heard about the border with Mexico, how Mexican officials were turning Americans away. "Even the end of the world is ironic," one of the men said, much to the amusement of his friends.

They'd gotten lucky: Not much gas was left at the station. No point in getting the underground tanks refilled, they were told. Soon, no one would be alive to need it. The men allowed Don and Rodney to fill the RV, and the extra canisters they had. When Rodney went to pay, the man behind the counter laughed at him. "What am I going to do with money?" he asked. "Not like I need it. You want granola bars? They're blueberry. I hate blueberry. Already ate all the chocolate ones, so."

They did not take the granola bars and thanked the men for the gas.

"Y'all be safe out there!" a man called after them, followed by hysterical laughter.

"Is it just me, or is everyone losing their minds?" Don asked when they were back in the RV.

"What do you expect them to do?" Rodney asked as the RV rumbled to life.

"Are we crazy?"

Rodney snorted. "Little late to be asking that, isn't it?"

Don changed tack. "Do you think anyone else is doing what we're doing?"

Rodney said, "I expect there's many people trying to set things right."

Thankfully, Rodney saw the girl first. Don was dozing in the seat next to him, not quite awake, not quite sleeping. He was in that hazy in-between space, the one where thoughts are sticky, muddled, translucent. The purr of the RV, the splattering remains of the storm, now a misty drizzle.

Then Rodney barked, "What the fuck?" and the RV shuddered as he slammed on the brakes.

Don's eyes shot open, heart rabbiting in his chest. He looked around wildly. Still in the RV. Rodney in the driver's seat. The windshield wipers going back and forth, back and forth.

"What is it?" Don asked breathlessly. "What's happened."

Rodney nodded. "Look."

Don followed his gaze out the front windshield. The sun was attempting to break through the clouds, the light weak. Around them, water dripped from old-growth trees, landing on ferns and underbrush.

In front of them, blacktop bisected by a faded yellow line. And there, lying in the middle of the road on her back, a woman.

Though, perhaps not quite a woman. She looked young, a girl on the verge of womanhood, her hair wet and plastered against the ground. She wore a yellow dress and white slippers that looked like they belonged to a ballerina. Her eyes were closed. Don couldn't tell if she was breathing or not.

"We have to help her," Don said, going for the door.

"Stop," Rodney snapped. Don looked at him. Rodney stared straight ahead at the girl in the road. A second ticked by. Then two. Then three. Then, "We don't know what's going on. It could be a trap."

"A trap? For what?"

"I don't know," Rodney said. He glanced at the side mirror. Don did the same out his own window. No one behind them. No people, no cars. Through the trees, the same. Nothing they could see aside from a wet forest. "We should just go."

"We can't leave her here," Don said. "She might be in trouble."

"She might be dead," Rodney countered.

They both screamed when the girl sat up and turned her head to look at them. She stood slowly, her soaked dress clinging against her slight frame. She brushed the hair hanging off her forehead to the side, and then lifted her other hand and waved, fingers wiggling. Her right eye was blackened, swollen. It looked as if she'd been punched in the face.

"Stay here," Rodney said, hand on the door handle.

"Not this time," Don said, and heard Rodney curse when he shoved open the door. The air was thick, moist. The mist coated Don's hair, his face. Rodney clambered out of the RV and joined Don at the front, the headlights momentarily hidden behind them. Don shivered as rain droplets landed on his exposed skin.

"Are you all right?" Rodney called to the girl, who was standing about fifteen feet down the road.

The girl said, "Are you real?"

Don gripped Rodney's hand.

"We're real," Rodney said. "Are you hurt? Do you need help?"

The girl said, "I want to go home. Can you please take me home?"

And then she put her face into her hands and began to sob.

Her name was Amelia, and she didn't want to be touched. When Don had tried to take her hand to lead her to the RV, she'd snatched it away, hissing at him like a feral cat, eyes wide and blazing. Don kept his distance after that.

They got her inside, gave her a towel. She dried off with it, slowly, mechanically, never losing the strange, shocked expression. When asked if she wanted to change out of her dress into something warmer, she refused. "This is my dress," she told them. "I made it. It took me three months. I pricked my finger with the needle. It bled. Don't worry about my eye. It's fine."

How old are you? they asked.

Eighteen, she told them. She'd just had her birthday two months before. There were balloons and cake and presents and music and friends and boys. She got a purple phone case for her phone, a new saddle for her horse. She was very happy with them, she said.

Where are your parents? they asked.

At home, she told them. They were waiting for her. Could they please give her a ride? She didn't want them to worry. She didn't have any money, but she was sure she could get some when they dropped her off.

"We don't need it," Rodney told her. "As long as we can get you home safe, that's payment enough."

Don agreed, but she made him uncomfortable. It had to be shock, the way she spoke: a flat monotone, all while barely blinking. Her face—heartbreakingly beautiful—looked like a mask, the skin pulled tight. But who was he to judge how people took the news about the end of the world?

They put her in the front, Don behind her on a bench seat where the small kitchen table folded out from the wall. He watched the back of her head. She never turned to look at them, always staring straight ahead, even when she began to talk. Every now and then, Rodney would glance in the rearview mirror, looking at Don. He got it too. Something was wrong. That feeling only intensified the longer she spoke.

Amelia said, "Two years ago, I met a boy. He was traveling with his family. They were from Maryland. He had green eyes, the color of grass. They came to the ranch because Daddy knows horses. He knows them so well. People come from all over and pay him to go riding in the hills. I help. Daddy taught me everything he knows. He said that if I wanted, the ranch would be mine, one day. I thought about that a lot. Did I want to stay here? Or did I want to explore? Could I do both? But I worried. What if I left and didn't want to come back? Would he love me any less? I didn't think so, but I'm their only kid. Mom and Daddy tried for another, but it wasn't meant to be. I wondered if I would end up resenting them if I stayed. Like I wasn't given the chance to go somewhere else. Turn left up here, please.

"The boy came, the boy with grass eyes. His name was Chris, and he'd just turned sixteen. He was so excited! He'd been on horses before, but never out in the open like this. His parents came too. They stayed for three days. On the second day, Chris and I went for a walk. It was sunny. He told me he wanted to hold my hand, but he was too nervous to try. I laughed at him but held his hand anyway. It was warm, smooth. City-boy hands. Mine were rough, callused. I liked the way it felt. He had long fingers and was always biting his nails. He said he wanted to live in a place like this. He was from a city and didn't like how loud it was. Sometimes, he said, he couldn't hear himself think. But out here, it was so quiet. Out here, it didn't feel like his brain was on fire.

"I didn't understand how powerful silence is. I liked the sounds of people in another room, a truck pulling up the driveway. The radio. The TV. Phones. Everything is loud all the time, and when you take that all away, it's so quiet. You can start to hear the blood moving in your body.

"We talked about so many things. He told me about his friends. How they went to the mall because no one else was ever there.

He told me about his school, much bigger than mine. He liked video games. And played basketball. His favorite food was tacos. He said they made good tacos at a place near his house. There were more people in his whole grade than at my school. He didn't know everyone, not like I did. And I thought that must be exciting. To see something new. To find people you hadn't seen every single day of your life. I told Chris I was scared of leaving, but he said that everyone was. You didn't know what was out there, but the more you pretended it didn't exist, the more left behind you got.

"I didn't want to be left behind. I wanted to live. I wanted to eat food that I'd never eaten before. Stay up until three in the morning, going from one party to the next. I wanted to hear the sounds of cars honking outside my window. I don't know why. Maybe as just a reminder that people are real. Out here, you don't get that. Everything is so quiet. You can hear yourself think. And sometimes, that little voice in your head says things you don't like. You're not good enough. You're not pretty enough. That birthmark on your hip is hideous. In the city, I bet it's too loud for thoughts. Keep going down this road.

"On his last day at the ranch, Chris told me he'd call. Text. Snapchat. And before he left, he kissed me under a willow tree. I'd never been kissed before. He tasted like mint gum and sweat and spit. I think it was good, for a first kiss. He didn't try and do more, just cupped my face and closed his eyes and went for it. His nose kept hitting mine. His tongue poked against my lips. I felt like I was on fire. It didn't last very long. Five seconds, maybe seven. I acted like such a little girl, blushing and playing with my hair. He looked proud of himself, like he'd been working up the courage to do that. I liked that about him. I waved goodbye to him as his family drove away. They were going to Joshua Tree. He said he'd send me pictures because I'd never been. I was sad, but not. It was exciting. I couldn't wait to see the pictures.

"He sent so many. I saved all of them. Some were of him, making faces. Others were of trees he liked, rocks in weird shapes. One had crystal in it. Quartz. He took it with him because he said he liked how pretty it was. He said he'd keep it safe because one day, he'd give it to me. I told him I loved it. Other pictures, with his mom and dad. With a boy he'd met and hung out with for most of a day. I can't remember the boy's name.

"He called me all the time. Sometimes it was only a minute or two. Other times, we'd be on the phone until past midnight. Me in my bed. Him in a hotel room, sitting on the toilet in the bathroom so he didn't wake his parents. We talked about everything. He loved movies. I loved books. He had a dog named Captain. I had a horse named Big Nose. He missed his grandma, who died last year. I told him I didn't know anyone who'd died. He said the funeral was terrible. He sniffled a little. I thought he was going to cry. He didn't. If he'd known me better, maybe he would have. I wouldn't have judged him. It's okay to cry when you feel like it.

"He didn't call me one day. Didn't text me back after a message that said good morning. I tried to call him, but there was no answer. I knew he was probably busy. Maybe his dad didn't like how much time he was spending on the phone. They were supposed to be on vacation, right? But I was sixteen. What did I know? I left a message. Sent some texts. Are you all right? What's going on? Did I do something wrong? Turn right up there. See it? Past the crooked tree.

"I spent that night being mad. I found a boy who liked me, and he wasn't talking to me. I yelled at Daddy for no reason. Mom too. They said that wasn't fair. It wasn't. I apologized but I was still angry. Why did he make a promise to me and then disappear? Was that how boys from cities were? Did they just take what they wanted and didn't think about how it made others feel? I didn't like that. It wasn't right. People shouldn't do that to other people.

"A week went by. And then another. And then another. I still thought about Chris all the time, but after the first few days, I didn't try to contact him anymore. I'd been ghosted. He disappeared like a ghost. It happens all the time. I read about it online. Boys do it, girls do it. I thought Chris was different. I thought he was better than that. I never heard from him again.

"Then Dad came to me about a month after Chris had left. Said he knew why Chris hadn't called me back, hadn't texted. He'd found an article online. I don't know why I hadn't thought to look him up by his name. I just didn't think about it. But Dad did. Chris and his parents were on their way back home. They were in the Blue Ridge Mountains, driving on a winding road. Another driver fell asleep at the wheel. He was in a tractor trailer. Hit them head-on. Chris and his parents died instantly. They'd already been put in the ground by the time I found out.

"I thought to myself, isn't that strange? One minute, you're riding horses and kissing under a willow tree, and the next, you're on a slab, waiting for someone to dig around your insides to confirm you died the way people thought you died, even though Chris apparently didn't have arms anymore, which, you know. My grandpa used to butcher pigs. Do you know how it's done? Hang them up by their bottom legs and slit their throats. A bucket underneath catches all the blood. Chris wasn't a pig. But they still stretched him out and caught all the blood that came from him. What a terrible thought that is. We're almost there. Keep going straight. See the cows? Those are ours.

"My parents said it was the way of things. That sometimes, when you least expect it, bad things can happen. It's not anyone's fault. It just was. And I remember thinking, how is that fair? How is that right? Was he scared? Did he see the truck coming? Or was he looking at the phone? Was he looking at his phone, scrolling through our messages, looking at the pictures we'd taken together?

Maybe if he hadn't been so distracted, he'd have seen the truck. Maybe he could have warned them. Daddy said it wasn't my fault. They probably went around a corner, and the truck was already in their lane. The truck driver wasn't hurt. Can he sleep at night? I wouldn't be able to.

"But I couldn't get one thought out of my head. Something my mom told me. She said at least he didn't suffer. That it was over probably before he felt any pain. I hoped that was true. If I had to go, I wouldn't want to suffer. I wouldn't want to know something was coming and that I couldn't do anything to stop it. Here one moment, happy, safe, and then gone the next without a thought of what had happened. Isn't that nice? Isn't that pretty?

"I wasn't okay for a long time. Which was weird. I knew him for a few weeks. In person, only a few days. I didn't know anything about him, really. But I was young, and more than halfway in love. How tragic, I told myself. I was like a girl in a book. A princess who loses her prince and her heart turns to stone. At least he didn't suffer. But I did. My heart didn't turn to stone. It was painful. It felt like I was being stabbed over and over again.

"We don't slaughter animals on the ranch. It's not that kind. But Daddy grew up on one that did. Cattle farm. They line them up in these pens that open up to narrow corridors they're funneled down. All in a row, all in a line. Then the cows are stunned with a gun. Not a normal gun, but with a metal bolt that hits the cows in the head, knocking them senseless. After they're stunned, they're hoisted up by their legs and their throats are cut. If you do it right, the cows won't know what's coming. That's what Daddy said.

"But I didn't believe him. I've known cows all my life. They're smart. A lot of them act like big puppies. They have *awareness.* You can see it in their eyes. There's the expression 'cow-eyed,' that means dull. Most cows aren't like that. They have personalities, wants, desires. Most of it is baser instinct, but it's still there. So yes, I think they suffered. I think they knew something was wrong when they got put in that pen. I think they knew something was wrong when they were shoved down the corridors. I think they heard what happened to the cows in front of them. Making noise and then . . . nothing. See the sign on the archway? Diamond K Ranch. That's us. Turn there.

"I never told my dad what I thought about the cows. How they knew what was coming. It didn't matter. Because six months after Chris died, the black hole came. And anytime you turned on the television, all those people losing their minds, police and military trying to push them back. Like cattle, all of them. And that's when I realized. *We're* the cattle. We're the cattle and we're being herded toward the narrow corridors. We know what's coming but there's nothing we can do to stop it. Soon, it's going to be our turn to be stunned and have our lives stolen from us. You can park right next to that SUV. It's not ours. People came to visit. There you go. Right there. Perfect. The people who came in the SUV were nice. They wanted to ride horses before the end of the world. A man and a woman. A couple. Their son. He was . . . eleven? Or maybe twelve years old.

"We have some people who work for us on the ranch. They live here too. We had ten of them. When the news came that we were all going to die, a few of them left. They wanted to see their families. But most stayed. They continued working. What else was there to do? Wail and scream? Try and run? No one's listening, and there's nowhere to go. So, they kept on working. Dad and Mom too. 'Someone's gotta do it,' Dad told me. 'Might as well be us.'

"I helped, but not as much as I used to. I was too caught up in what was going on. I'd never really thought about black holes before. Why would I? I didn't care about space. I could see stars anytime I wanted to. There are people who dream of flying, seeing the curve of the Earth. I like my feet on the ground, thank you very much. I sat at the computer for hours and hours and hours, reading everything I could. Some people thought it was going to be over in an instant, that we wouldn't even have time to react. Others thought that we were going to feel every single part of it. That our skin will melt. The blood in our veins would boil. Radiation poisoning, if we weren't dead from a blast of invisible energy. I hated that thought. I didn't want anyone I loved to suffer. What if we survived, but my father's tongue fell out of his mouth? What if my mother lost her lips, her eyes, her ears? What if her skin only partially melted, and she looked like a monster? She would be in so much pain, begging for someone to help her, and what could we do? Nothing, I think. Nothing aside from helping her sleep.

"I wanted to help them. I wanted to save them. I didn't want them to suffer. Chris didn't suffer. Did I tell you that? Mom said he didn't, and I wanted that for them. I didn't want them sitting in front of the television at night, seeing how hopeless things were getting. I wanted them to be happy. To remember the life we'd built. See the barn? Daddy built that before I was born. It took four months. Everyone chipped in because people care about each other. Most of us want to see others succeed.

"But I couldn't shake the thought that they were going to melt, that they were going to suffer. I couldn't stand the thought of my mother screaming in pain because her skin was boiling. I couldn't stand the thought of my father with burnt-out eyes and nothing on his mind but dying. When you're in pain, when you're *suffering*, all you want to do is make it stop. You *wish* for death. They were suffering. I could see it in their eyes. The lines on their foreheads. The secret conversations they had. They were my parents. I needed to protect them. They were wishing, but they couldn't say it out loud.

"Living on a ranch, you learn things. All the chores that need doing because there are always chores. How to ride. How to mend fences and cattle guards. You learn to use machines, tools. What to watch for in case your animals get sick. How to shovel manure. How to clean stalls. How to care for the saddles, the bit. How to herd cows. And if an animal hurts itself, beyond fixing, you do the merciful thing. You put them down. It was Mom who taught me how to shoot. She was better than Dad. He loved that about her. No one could hit a target like my Mom. She had this rifle. It was her granddad's. She cared for it, kept it clean and oiled. It was the first gun I learned to shoot. It was big. It hurt when the stock slammed against my shoulder. But my mom was there, right behind me, and when I fired that first shot when I was six, she cheered for me, even though I'd missed the target. We were only ten feet away, but you would have thought I hit the bull's-eye with how happy she was. She looked so wonderful in that moment. I can remember it like it happened yesterday.

"I didn't have my own gun. We had plenty. Rifles. Pistols. A shotgun to scare off coyotes. They were stored away in a gun cabinet, which was locked. But the key was always sitting in the bowl near the back door. Anyone could use it if they wanted to.

"I couldn't take it anymore. I couldn't let them suffer. I took one of the guns. A Glock 9. It uses nine-millimeter bullets. I checked to make sure it wasn't loaded first. Daddy said that a gun can load itself when you're not looking, so you always have to check. The magazine was empty. Standard-capacity magazine for the Glock 9 holds fifteen bullets. I loaded up each and every one.

"I used thirteen of them. When most everyone was out in the fields, I called one of the ranch hands into the barn. I told him I needed help with something. His name was Bill. Good guy. Older, had been on the ranch for almost fifteen years. Always smiling. I shot him in the back of the head so he wouldn't suffer. It wasn't as loud as I expected it to be. He fell down and didn't move. I put some sawdust around him to keep the blood from spreading. And then I called for the next ranch hand. And the next. All seven of them. Not a single one knew what was coming because I didn't want them to suffer. I wanted them to leave before they could. I don't think they saw the other bodies before they died.

"Mom and Dad came back. I was in the house. They were early. I thought I had more time. They asked where everyone was. I said I had something to tell them. We sat at the kitchen table. I told them I was scared. That I didn't like the idea of waiting. It felt bad. Why wait for something that's going to hurt? Why should we just sit here and not take matters into our own hands? Why are you looking at me like that? Don't be afraid. Don't be sad.

"Dad went first. Then Mom. They didn't have a chance to react. Boom, boom, and then they lay down at the table and went to sleep. I didn't want to track sawdust through the house, so I put down towels. It didn't work very well, but I felt better. See what I'd done? I'd helped them. I'd kept them from suffering. Like Chris, it was over in an instant. I spent the rest of the day lying in my bed and listening to birds out the open window. I slept a little and when I woke up, I'd forgotten my parents were dead, but only for a couple of minutes. They're still inside, where I left them. They don't look like they used to, not anymore. It smells bad too.

"I tried to use the gun on myself. I put the barrel against my head and counted to ten. By the time I got to six, I was already putting pressure on the trigger. But by the time I got to ten, I couldn't go through with it. I don't know why. I didn't want to suffer. I didn't want to be here when the fire came. I didn't want my skin to melt off, or the marrow in my bones to boil. So why couldn't I do it?

"I called the police three days later. No one answered. I called again. And again. And again. Finally, at about one in the morning, someone picked up. He said he was a deputy. He was crying.

I asked him what was wrong. He said he was so scared. That he didn't want the world to end. I told him I understood, and that I had killed my parents. Could he please come and arrest me? He laughed at me. He laughed at me and said that it didn't matter, not anymore. And then he hung up on me.

"The next morning, a family came. I had forgotten to check the reservations. Everyone else had canceled, so why hadn't they? They pulled up in their SUV. The boy came out first. He was so excited. He had wanted to ride horses all his life. They were supposed to stay in the house with us. Like before, when other people did it. He said he'd been reading about our ranch. Was it true we had twelve horses? Was it true we had hundreds of cows?

"We did. I told him as much. I asked him if he'd like to see them. He said yes. His parents said they wanted to take pictures before coming into the barn. I told them not to go inside the house because the floors had just been mopped for their arrival. It needed time to dry.

"I almost couldn't do it. The boy was so happy. I thought he'd burst out of his skin. He couldn't see the others. I had put hay on top of them. The smell wasn't bad. It smelled like a farm with something sweet on top, like newly spoiled meat. But then I thought about Chris, and how he didn't suffer. I thought about the ranch hands. My parents. I was doing the merciful thing. He didn't make a sound as he fell. His parents must have heard the shot because they started yelling, asking us if we were all right. I told them yes, we were, but their son had tripped. Could they come in and help?

"They did. They came running. I thought that was strange. What did it matter if it happened now or three weeks from now? It was all going to be the same end. The dad got there first and though I tried to keep him from seeing inside, he did. He started screaming. I couldn't have that. Boom, and down he went. The mother came in only a few seconds later. She didn't go for her husband or her son. She went after me. I was startled. She didn't make a sound. Punched me in the eye, and I fell back against one of the pens. The gun went off. Boom, that was bullet number twelve going into the barn floor. She didn't stop. Her lips were pulled back over her teeth. I'd never seen a person look like an animal before, not like that. Her eyes were . . . black. She looked like a monster. I almost dropped the gun. She came for me again, boom, down she went. Thirteen bullets. Two left.

"I didn't know where to go. I didn't want to stay at the house because my parents were swelling. I couldn't stay in the barn because the floor was sticky. So I just started walking and walking and walking and then I got so tired, I lay down on the ground. Rain fell on my face, my lips. It was cold. I let it fall in my mouth, my throat. And then you two came and found me and now I'm here. I still have the gun. See? It's right here. Funny thing, isn't it? Not very big. Two bullets left. I could have put more in, but I didn't think I needed to. Plenty enough for one more person. But, for some reason, I still can't do it. I still can't pull the trigger. Thank you for the ride. I really appreciate it. Would you like me to help you? A bullet for each of you. We can even go into the barn. It's nice in there. Quiet. You can hear yourself think, even if the thoughts aren't very nice.

"I know what's going on in your head. I can see it on your faces. She's crazy, you're thinking. She's out of her mind. But that's not right. I'm thinking more clearly than I ever have before. Maybe that's what I'm meant to do. Help others like yourself to keep you from suffering. If I can't do it to myself, then at the very least, I can do it for others. Would you like that? Do you want me to ease your suffering?"

She looked at them with dead eyes—*cow eyes*, Don thought hysterically, the Glock 9 sitting in her lap, her finger on the trigger.

She'd pulled it from a pocket in her dress. Don couldn't move, didn't think he'd taken a breath since halfway through her story. Rodney's back was pressed against the driver's door, his body twisted so that he faced Amelia. If he reached for her from behind, she could still get off a shot. If Rodney went for her, same result. He believed her when she said she knew how to use it.

Sweat trickled down his brow, the only sound coming from the cooling *tick tick tick* of the RV's engine. He almost didn't believe it, that this girl had killed her parents, others. Twelve people in total, if she was telling the truth. But then, she had a gun, so why wouldn't she be?

Rodney said, "I appreciate the offer." His voice was slow, even. "It's very kind of you to suggest something like that, but my husband and I can't stay. We have somewhere to be."

"Where?" she asked in that same flat tone. Never once had there been any emotion the entire time she'd spoken. It was like she'd been reciting a story she was almost bored by. Shock, yes, but it went much further than that, much deeper. Something in her had been destroyed beyond repair.

"Away," Rodney said. "We made a promise to someone, and we need to keep it."

"Like Chris did?" she asked, staring at the farmhouse.

Rodney nodded. "Exactly like Chris. You know he wanted to keep on talking to you. I bet it was the only thing he thought about after he left."

"I like that," she said. "It's nice to think about. It's stupid, you know? I barely knew him." She brushed a thumb over the gun's grip.

"That doesn't matter," Rodney said. "When you know, you know. It's not fair what happened. To him or to you. But it did. It happened. Nothing can change that."

"I know," she said. She opened the passenger door, causing Don to jump. "Would you like to see the barn? We have horses."

"No," Rodney said firmly, the skin under his right eye twitching. "Thank you for the offer, but we need to get back on the road."

She hesitated, her hand tightening around the gun. "Are you sure? I don't want you to suffer."

"Suffering is life," Rodney said. "It's part and parcel of living. It never really goes away, but you can become bigger around it. Stronger. The things you thought you weren't capable of are easier than you think."

She stared at him for a long moment, still halfway out of the RV. "I like you," she said eventually. "I don't want you to feel pain. Get out and come to the barn."

"I can't," Rodney said gently. "But if you'd like to go in there, you can. No one here will try and stop you."

Her face screwed up, and Don thought she was going to cry. She didn't, and a moment later, the tight mask returned. "Thank you for the ride. You have been so nice to me. My mother's face is blue and purple now. Maybe I should try and call the police again?"

"Do that," Rodney said. "Keep calling until someone listens. They will."

"You promise?" she asked.

"Yes," Rodney said.

"Okay. I can do that. I will go inside and call the police over and over until someone listens to me. You promised they would, so I hope that's true." She looked back at Don. "Do you want to go to the barn?"

"No," he whispered, hand shaking.

"I didn't think you would," she said. "Goodbye." She closed the door and began to walk toward the house. She didn't flinch when Rodney started the RV.

"Keep an eye on her," Rodney snapped, looking at the side mirrors.

The RV began to reverse quickly down the driveway. Don watched Amelia. She reached the front porch steps. She looked at the barn. Looked at her gun. Tilted her head back to look at the sky. Then she turned and began to wave. Through the partially open driver's window, they could hear her shouting. "Thank you for visiting the Diamond K Ranch! Come back soon!"

And then she sat on the steps and bowed her head. The gun hung loosely from her fingers between her legs.

Rodney spun the wheel. The RV lurched dangerously, clouds of dust billowing up around them. He put the RV into drive and shot down the driveway. In the side mirror, Don saw her face, her yellow dress before they crested a hill. After that, she was gone.

Rodney cursed up a storm the farther they got from the ranch. Spitting mad, as Don liked to say. He kept glancing in the side mirror, as if he thought Amelia would be coming after them. Maybe in the SUV. She would have access to it now. Don stared straight ahead, hands flat on his lap.

It didn't take them long to find the road they'd been on when they'd stumbled across Amelia. From start to finish, they'd only been with her under an hour, but Don was sore, tense, as if he'd just been in the trenches. When Amelia had revealed the gun—still talking, talking, talking in that flat voice of hers—he'd panicked. There were knives in the drawer just across from him. An electric teakettle in one of the cabinets. He'd thought about grabbing it and bringing it down on her head. He hadn't, but it'd been a close thing.

A half hour later, Rodney pulled the RV off the road, using the emergency lights even though they hadn't seen anyone else since

Amelia. He closed his eyes and laid his head against the steering wheel.

Eventually, he said, "That was . . ."

"I know."

"I believed her."

"So did I."

"She . . ."

"Yes."

Rodney's eyes were wet when he lifted his head. A rare occurrence for the stoic man. Don could count on both hands the number of times he'd seen Rodney cry. He wasn't quite there yet, but close enough. "Could we have helped her?"

"I don't think so," Don said quietly. He'd climbed into the passenger seat shortly after they'd escaped. Now, he reached over and took Rodney's hand in his. Rodney's wedding ring glinted in the low light. "She was already gone."

"I thought . . ." His throat worked. "I saw her doing it. Walking us into the barn, telling us that it was all going to feel better soon. I can't—Can you imagine what that must have felt like for the others? Not knowing what they were walking into."

"It wouldn't have felt like anything at all," Don said. "Something they always did, probably."

Rodney slammed his hand against the steering wheel. "Her parents. A *kid*."

"I know."

"Jesus Christ," he muttered, blinking rapidly.

Don rubbed his hands together to try and stop them from shaking. "What do we do? We can't go back, but we can't just leave her out there on her own."

Rodney's eyes were dry now. A little red, but dry. "Yes, we can. And we're going to. I'm not going back out there. She's armed. We're lucky enough as it is."

"But—"

"Donald."

He sighed. "I know. I know." His thoughts were jumbled, Amelia's voice whispering in his head. He wondered if he'd ever sleep again. Not that it would matter for long, but still. "Why is this happening?"

"Would it make you feel better if there was an answer to that? An explanation for everything bad that happens?"

He knew what Rodney was saying, what he was talking about. Not just Amelia. Not just the end of the world. It was more than that. They were getting ever closer to *him*.

"Yes," Don said. "I think it would. I know that's not how the world works. We can know when and how and where, but the *why*? That's what haunts me. You can be surrounded by people who love you, who want what's best for you, and it's still not enough. Because there's something inside some people that eats up everything good. All the light." He paused, stomach slick and oily. "Some people have black holes in them. They try and escape, they try and break free, but it's too strong. Burns up everything until there's nothing left but ash. And what does that mean for the rest of us? If we get too close, we run the risk of getting caught in the pull. But if we do nothing, what does that make us?"

"It's not the same."

"Bullshit it's not," Don snapped. "You saw the look in her eyes. Don't tell me it didn't remind you of—"

"It *didn't*," Rodney retorted, cheeks splotchy. "He was nothing like her."

"I'm not saying he was. I'm saying that they couldn't ignore what's in them. It took them, it changed them, made them mean and cold and nonsensical. Makes them paranoid, distrusting. And when you pile on *this*?" He jabbed a finger toward the sky. "It's a wonder we're all not more broken than we already are. How the hell do we go on every day knowing this is reality?"

Rodney said, "We do it regardless."

"What?"

"We do it regardless," Rodney repeated. "We go on because we know what we're supposed to do. We go on because we have to. I can't just stop. I can't just let it go. Not now. Not when it's the most important thing we've ever done. Should we have done it sooner? Yes. We should have. But we couldn't because we know what seeing him again means. We know what this last part is. We made a promise and we still have time."

"I'm scared," Don admitted.

Rodney lifted Don's hand, kissing his palm once, twice. "I know. I am too. But we've made it this far. Might as well see it through to the end." He looked away. "But I can't do it by myself. I need you."

Rare, this, coming from him. Don knew he was loved, knew it to the moon and back, but every now and then, Rodney would talk like this. Pointed. Direct. *Real.* It was one of the million reasons Don cared so deeply for him. Sometimes, people saw Rodney just as he appeared: a quiet, somewhat ornery old man. He was more. So much more.

"Can we do it?"

"We've made it this far," he said again.

"I suppose we have."

Rodney turned off the emergency blinkers, flipped the single indicator—even though the road was empty—and began to drive away.

CHAPTER 5

Strangely, driving into Montana—one of the least populated states—proved to be difficult. Many smaller roads had been blocked off. Ranches, farms, neighborhoods where people stood in front of barriers with guns. They didn't look like police or military. Just people. They didn't speak, just shouldered their guns if anyone tried to approach. A few tried and were rebuffed. No shots were fired.

More people, more cars. Four lanes of traffic—two east and two west. Slow going, maybe a mile every ten minutes. It was while they were stuck just across the border from South Dakota that Don decided to hear what was new.

He flipped on the radio, spinning the dial until he found a news station. It wasn't coming in all that clear, but they could make out the words. The first thing they heard: Jupiter had been destroyed. Images from NASA showed the big planet had broken into five large chunks, the biggest the size of a hundred earths. All were being pulled toward the black hole. There was no risk of any part of Jupiter's remains hitting Earth. Small favors.

Three weeks. That's what they'd initially thought was left. But now, given the swift destruction of Jupiter, it looked as if things were speeding up. Perhaps fifteen days left. Perhaps ten.

The Man in Charge spoke next. According to the reporter, he had not been seen publicly or heard from in nearly a week. The last time anyone had heard from him was when he'd condemned the rioting, the looting, the destruction. He spoke from an undisclosed location. He said that he wished things could be different. That he never expected this to happen. No one did, he mused. It caught them all by surprise, and though they'd known about the black hole for close to two years (neglecting to mention the public wasn't made aware until a full year after the discovery), they'd hoped it could be stopped. His faith, he told the listening audience, was now more important than ever. His relationship with God had never been stronger, as was his belief in a Heaven for those deserving. He prayed, he said, prayed for hours and hours. He didn't get a reply as that's not how God worked. Instead, he was overcome with a strange sense of calm. He called it part of the grief process, and he'd reached acceptance.

"For billions of years, this planet has survived. What was once molten rock gave way to land, to oceans. And from those oceans, the first hint of life. It evolved. It grew. It grew until eventually, we came. We've only been here for a fraction of the Earth's life. In the grand scheme of things, we're a grain of sand on an infinite beach. But we mattered. All of us. For better or worse, we mattered. We made music. We wrote books. Machines that chased stars. We created civilizations. We followed religions. We built. We destroyed. We loved. We killed. We started wars." He paused. "*I* started wars. I did that. I sent your children to die in faraway places, all in the name of preserving peace. Most of you will never forgive me, and I understand why. It seems almost pointless, now, doesn't it? With what's coming, earthly desires, earthly complaints, none of it seems important. I wrestle with the idea constantly. I worry about the people who don't have my faith. What must they think is coming after? I worry about the people who *do* share my faith. What if we're wrong?

"I don't think I am, but there is a sliver of doubt. Funny how that works. My faith—especially now—should be absolute. I know the glory of the kingdom of God. I know He will welcome us with open arms and we will only know peace and light. But then doubt creeps in, gnawing at the faith. Chipping away at it. Cracking it. Breaking it apart. If there is a God, if there is a higher power, why is He letting this happen? Why is he sitting idly by while the hour of our ending approaches?

"I don't have an answer to that. I wish I did. It would make me—and, I suspect, many others—not afraid. But that hasn't happened. So it's left to us. The people. I don't know what's going to happen. Maybe three weeks from now, the entirety of Earth's life and history will be gone. That does not change what we did while here. Good and bad. We made choices, decisions that reverberated throughout the world.

"Last night, I looked at the moon for hours. When was the last time you gave any real thought about the moon outside of a landing or an eclipse? When it's full, we exclaim how big it is, how bright. But like everything else, we see it, and it passes through our minds with no resistance. Then it's gone until the next time we see it. Isn't that funny? An orbiting body that affects the tides, the tilt of the earth, and we just . . . take it for granted. It's beautiful, really. I will miss it when it's gone, in the few short hours we have left. I spoke with the remaining crew on the International Space Station just this morning. I asked them about the moon. They said it was even more beautiful up close. They will stay on the ISS until the end.

"And now, a promise: I will speak to you every day around this same time. Experts say that satellite interference won't occur until the final few days, so I'll do my best to let you hear me, to give you the most up-to-date information that is available. If possible, stay in your homes. Avoid any and all roadways. All flights have been grounded, all ships docked. The military has been deployed to major metropolitan areas around the country to ensure the safety of the populace. They have orders to shoot on sight if anyone attempts to disregard their instructions. I did not make this decision lightly. Even if the world falls, that does not give anyone the right to take the law into their own hands. But I am asking you as your leader: The people deployed to protect our interests do not deserve to be forced to take a life on American soil. Please do not force their hands.

"May God bless you. May God bless these United States. And may God bless each and every single one of our souls."

"The Stars and Stripes Forever" began to play. Such a grating sound.

Don turned off the radio. They'd barely moved five feet since the Man in Charge had started speaking.

Rodney said, "Faith. What a bunch of bullshit. Did you hear that asshole? As if *God* is the answer and reason for everything. They love Him even now. Even as they beg for answers. Trust in His plan, they say. When bad things happen, they happen for a *reason*. That's a cop-out. Bad things don't happen because of some infinite force pulling the strings, but because of sheer, rotten luck. Nothing, and I mean *nothing* can stand against luck. Random happenstance. Chance. *That* is the higher power. That is the altar of reality. Everything is chaos and when and if things happen, it all comes down to luck."

Don said, "You never believed in fate."

Rodney snorted. "No. You and me? We weren't destined to be. We're here because we worked for it. We worked hard. We survived some of the worst things people can live through. It's not fate. It was you and me who did it. No one and nothing else."

Someone honked their horn a few cars behind them. As if that would help. As if that would make anyone move.

"What does it matter then?" Don asked. "Why does any of this matter if it's all down to luck? We get up every morning not knowing if today is going to be the best day of our lives or the worst. But we still get up because we have to."

"Not everyone," Rodney said, and Don felt like screaming. Close, so close. They were getting back there, to that space, to that land where everything was made of shattered glass. They'd been there before—brief visits, as much as grief would allow—but it'd been a while. Not because they'd forgotten. How could they?

It was because it made everything hurt. It made Don feel like a failure. Like he could have—and should have—done more. That was the crux of it: Had they done enough? They were told they had by so many people. Friends. Family. Doctors. But in the end, it hadn't been enough. It just hadn't.

Don said, "That's not fair." It came out harsh, angry. His throat began to close as his eyes burned.

Rodney sighed, looking as old as Don had ever seen him. "No, I don't suppose that was. I just . . ." He swallowed thickly. "I'm trying to make sense out of the nonsensical. My head feels like it's exploding every waking minute. I can't sleep very well. Food tastes like nothing. I don't understand anything anymore."

"You're old," Don said with a sniff. "That's to be expected."

Rodney made a face. "Don't you start in on that again."

"Your blood pressure is high."

"So what? Not like it matters now."

"You have an enlarged prostate."

"I'm gay," Rodney said, deadpan. "It helps."

Don didn't want to laugh. He wanted to stay angry. He wanted to have this out. But he laughed. Of course he did. To most, Rodney was slightly dour, a little grumpy. Don thought he was one of the funniest people he'd ever known. Yes, he was biased, but no one could make him laugh like Rodney.

"You're terrible," Don said as he chuckled. "Just awful."

"I am aware, yes."

The vehicles in front of them began to inch forward once more.

"We're all lost," Don said. "I think we go through most of life feeling that way. But now? With all of this? It's exponential, to a point."

"What do you mean?"

"It can only go so far. I think we're reaching the peak. I don't know why, but I'm feeling . . . calmer? Calmer than I have in days. Even with all we've seen in the last weeks, all we've heard, I'm getting calmer, not more scared." He paused. "It's almost like I've been infected by the hippies."

Rodney tapped his hands against the steering wheel. "It's the inevitability. We know there's nothing we can do to change it. It's almost like acceptance, I guess. You know what I've noticed? Cell phones."

"What about them?"

"Look at the people out there," Rodney said, nodding toward the windshield. "See the people standing outside? See the people in their cars? You pass by people, and their heads are always down, looking at their phones. Always on their phones when they're driving, when they're walking, when they're eating or on the shitter or watching TV. That little magic rectangle filled with everything known to mankind. All of our history. Everything we've learned. It's all there. But no one's looking at their phones anymore. Not really. It's like it took the end of the world for people to look up and see each other."

"Amelia," Don said.

"She saw people too," Rodney said darkly. "But in a different way than most people. We aren't good, Don. We aren't bad, either. We just *are*, like most people. We've done things right. We've done things wrong. We've made catastrophic mistakes. But we're not like Amelia. We have purpose."

"She did too," Don said. "Or she thought she did. Does that make her any more right or wrong than we are?"

"Well, yes, Don. We didn't kill people."

"When you put it like that, I suppose you're right."

They sat in traffic for a long time.

Swan Lake in Montana, with waters so clear the stones resting on the lakebed were visible. They'd been here before. Not quite in this area, but close. Bigfork wasn't too far away, along with an even bigger lake: Flathead.

Something was wrong with the sky. As dusk settled, the reds and oranges of a sunset did not appear: rather, the sky was a shifting mixture of violet, green, and a blue so dark it almost looked black. One could be forgiven if they thought it was the aurora borealis. It wasn't; the space anomaly had done something to the light in the sky, making it look surreal, as if from a dream.

The moon was full, bright. Don thought about what the Man in Charge had said, how he hadn't given much thought to the moon beyond it being in the sky. That had all changed, and Don wondered why he'd never really thought about it before, not like that. When had he lost the curiosity and wonder found in youth? Did it disappear with the cynicism that comes with age? He'd spent so much time with his head down, trying to get through life. Now, he never wanted to look away from the sky again.

They weren't alone. The campground by the lake wasn't full, but there were plenty of people around: some in cars, some in trucks, some in RVs bigger than Don and Rodney's. Tents had been set up and fires were going. Music played from multiple different directions: country music, oldies, classical. To their left, Garth Brooks sang. To their right, Run-DMC. In the distance: someone had an electric keyboard and was playing "Clair de Lune." That song again.

Don and Rodney had kept their distance. Some had waved at them as they'd gotten out of the RV, but most minded their own business.

Until the two young women came over.

They were sitting in ratty folding chairs. Canned soup on the fire. Chicken noodle. Warm juice. Slightly stale bread. A feast of champions. Don didn't mind.

"Looks like we're about to have company," Rodney said quietly, and Don looked up beyond the fire.

The women appeared to be in their early twenties. One had long hair, the other's cropped close to her skull, almost militarily so. Their hands were joined between them.

Don waved in greeting. "Hello, there."

The woman with short hair spoke first. "Hi! We saw you over here and wanted to come say hello."

"So," the other woman said. "Hello."

"I'm Amy. This is Becca."

"Rodney," Don said, pointing at his husband. "And I'm Don."

Amy smiled at them. "It's nice to meet you. Forgive me for being forward, but I saw you two kiss when you arrived. It's nice to meet other queer people on the road."

Becca rolled her eyes. "Just right out there with it. Spied on you two macking on each other, and now we're here. Good job, Ames."

"Gay," Rodney said. "I don't know about all the queer stuff."

"He's not fond of that word," Don said. "We've heard it spat in anger and vitriol more times than we can count."

"You can reclaim it all you like," Rodney said, arms crossed. "And I won't ever stop you from using it, but it can still be hard to hear sometimes. Also, I do not *mack*. Anything I do is with purpose."

"I don't think that's quite what she meant," Don said, patting his arm.

Rodney scowled at all of them. "Any lingo I've learned in the last twenty years has been against my will."

"I love them," Amy breathed.

"Oh dear god," Becca said with a sigh. "Sorry about her. She's just . . . exuberant."

"So is he," Don said as Rodney snorted. "Would you like to sit? We don't have any more chairs, but you're welcome to enjoy the fire."

"Thanks," Amy said, plopping down on the ground on the other side of the fire. She kicked off her sandals, pointing her feet toward the flames. "Sorry if I seem all over the place. I have ADHD and ran out of meds. Thought I'd stockpiled enough, but." She shrugged. "You know how it goes. You can't really plan for the end of the world."

"Ain't that the truth." Becca grunted as she sat down next to Amy. She peered at them over the top of the flickering fire. "We haven't met older people like us. Queer elders, you know?"

Rodney barked out a laugh. "Elders. Good lord."

"She's not wrong," Don told him. He looked back at the women. "How long have you two been together?"

Becca and Amy glanced at each other for a long moment. "Since we were fourteen. Almost ten years now."

"Goodness," Don said. "That's quite a long time for being so young."

Amy beamed at them. "When you know, you know. She transferred into our school in Texas. I was smitten almost immediately. She didn't like me at first."

"Cheerleader," Becca said, like she was proud. "Jock boyfriend. Preacher dad. The whole nine yards. Little Miss Americana."

"And then you corrupted me," Amy said gleefully.

"You're damn right I did. Didn't take much, either."

Amy looked at Don and Rodney. "It was almost like deprogramming. You know what some people have to go through when they leave a cult? It was like that. Only this cult was Texas Christianity. I grew up being taught that a woman needed to find a husband as soon as possible. A woman's place was in the home, making sure it was kept neat and orderly for her husband when he arrived from work. Get loaded up with three children, church every Sunday and voilà! You have the life of every woman in my family going back generations."

"She was almost there, too," Becca said. "Her father was already talking about her wedding, how she was going to make a God-fearing wife and mother."

"At fourteen," Amy said, shaking her head. "Can you imagine what that's like? In so many words, being told that you're essentially breeding stock. I'll tell you what, though. Getting finger-blasted the first time by a girl was certainly eye-opening."

"Jesus Christ," Rodney muttered.

"Sorry!" Amy squeaked as she slammed a hand over her mouth. "I didn't mean to say it like that! I meant that she changed so much, things I didn't even know *could* be changed."

"Did you get found out?" Don asked.

Becca sighed. "Of course we did. When you're that age, you think everything you're doing is smart. And you get so wrapped up in it that you forget someone is always watching."

"Daddy took me to church," Amy said, picking up a fallen leaf and beginning to shred it. "A bunch of other people were there from the congregation. They prayed over me for hours. Just kept going on and on and on. Talking about how I was hiding myself from the light of God. That I was turning away from Him. That if I returned, if I admitted my sins and turned away from them, all would be forgiven. They put their hands on my face, my shoulders, my arms, my legs. They tried to hold me down at one point, but

I screamed and screamed. One of them—this old man with bad breath and bony fingers—told my father that I was possessed by the devil."

"A *lesbian* devil," Becca said, and Don smiled at the fierce pride in her voice.

"I stopped fighting," Amy said. "I knew it was the only way out. So I pretended. I said that I heard God. That He spoke in me. He loved me, I told them. He loved me and wanted me to be in His image. I repented right then and there." She leaned forward, shadows dancing across her face. "But it was all a lie."

"Why?" Rodney asked.

She shrugged. "Because I had this thought. I don't know why I hadn't considered it before, but when it hit me, it was all I could think about. We're taught that God made us. That we are, in essence, His children. And like all parents, He was going to be disappointed in me a lot, but nothing that couldn't be forgiven if you wanted it bad enough. But I kept thinking, well, if God didn't want me to be this way, why am I? If God thinks being queer is so terrible, why did He make it so we could *be* that? That's when I realized the truth."

"Which is?" Don asked.

Amy laughed. "God's not real. And even if He is, why would He give a shit about me having a girlfriend? It doesn't make any sense! The Bible isn't His thoughts, His words. Every single line in the Good Book is man-made. Interpretations passed down through generations like the world's worst game of telephone. *And*," she added, "queer people existed long before the Bible ever did. I mean, come on. There are queer whales! Queer lions! Surely, *they're* part of God's Plan, so why do they bone each other and we're not allowed?"

"Succinct as usual," Becca said.

"What happened with your father?" Don asked.

Amy looked away, jaw tense. "He found us again. A few months later, right after my fifteenth birthday. He threatened to send me away to a camp. Not the kind with crafts and swimming in a lake. The conversion kind. The worst kind. They still exist in Texas. Other places, too. You know what they do in places like those?"

Rodney nodded. "We've heard stories."

"We ran," Becca said. "Right then and there. Got on a bus and headed north. They tried to look for us, but we stayed one step ahead of them. Rough few years. Slept in the car a lot. Stayed in shelters. Found ourselves in Maryland. Got a shitty room to sublet. Got jobs. Our GEDs."

"A good life," Amy said. "The best life. God, do you remember that room? No hot water. No air-conditioning. A tiny window that only opened a crack. But it was ours. I loved it so much. I put up decorations. Plants. Rainbow flags. Little pillows I got from Goodwill to put on the bed to make it look fancy."

"You did a great job," Becca told her, kissing the side of her head. "I loved that home."

"Did you ever see your parents again?" Don asked.

"Once," Amy said. "Right after my twenty-first birthday. I was working as a waitress at a nice restaurant. Good tips. I liked it. One night, the hostess told me people had requested to be seated in my section. It was my dad, and other people from the church."

"She didn't tell me about it until she got home," Becca said, glaring at the fire. "I wasn't very happy about that, but I got over it because Amy can handle herself."

"I can," she said with a sniff. "And I did. I went over to them, and it felt like I was floating through a dream. As soon as my dad saw me, he grabbed my arm and said he was going to take me home. So I did the best thing I could."

"Which was?" Rodney asked.

"I screamed that a man was touching me without my permission," Amy said. "I screamed at him to let me go, that a *stranger* was trying to hurt me. I'd been there for almost a year. I'd made friends, especially with the guys in the kitchen. They loved me. I loved them. They treated me like I was one of the boys. So when they heard me screaming, they all came running out. He tried to say that he was my dad, that he was *entitled* to do with me whatever he wanted. So I lied. I said I'd never seen this man before in my life. It wasn't the first lie I'd told, or the last. But it was the one that made me feel the most powerful. There was nothing he could do to prove anything. They forced him out and I never saw him again. He did send a letter to the restaurant, a few months later. I didn't read it. Instead, I took a lighter from one of the cooks and burned it in the parking lot. Maybe it was him apologizing. Maybe it was him telling me that he'd been wrong all my life, and that he wanted nothing more than to love me like a father should." She shook her head. "I didn't need to read it to know it'd be filled with scripture and quotes about ungrateful children and returning to the light. But even if it *had* been conciliatory, fuck him. Fuck him and his God that teaches hate and bigotry, all in the name of Christ."

"Do you have any regrets?" Don asked.

She stared at him hard. "What would I regret? I escaped a prison and found all the color in the world. I've seen meteor showers. I've touched buffalo and bison. A few years ago, I read something about buried treasure hidden in the Appalachians and spent months dragging Becca around to look for it. We never found anything, but that didn't matter. What matters is that I'm able to make my own choices. What matters is I survived. What matters is I flourished. Not because of my parents or where I came from, but despite them. *To* spite them. The best revenge any queer person can get is to be happy. It took me a while to realize that, but when I did, I'd never felt so free."

"And we found others like us," Becca said. "So many others. Queer people. People like us, people not like us but loving all the same. So much is discussed around the idea of found family. But what most people don't realize is that queer people *made* that. A lot of us aren't born to people who will love their children like they should, so we have to go out and make families of our own. We did that. We found people who loved us for who we are. And no matter what happens next, no one can take that away from us."

"And now you want to talk to the old gays," Rodney said.

"Elders," Amy corrected gently. "In this house, we show respect."

Rodney groaned as Don laughed. "That's . . . kind of you. I think?"

Amy ducked her head as she smiled. "I like people. Some of them. I don't know. It's weird, right? We all have mostly the same innards, but some people act like their family tree is a circle. I don't get it." Then, with barely a pause to suck in a quick breath, she asked, "Do you like being old? I'll never get to be. Isn't that crazy? Just wow. Wow. That's a weird thought. I want to know what it's like."

"Amy," Becca said, obviously embarrassed. "You can't just—"

Surprisingly, it was Rodney who spoke. "It's fine. I don't . . . I'm sorry for that."

Amy blinked. "For what?"

"That you'll never know what it's like to grow old. While it's not all that it's cracked up to be, I guess it's not all bad."

"Not bad at all," Don said. He looked at Rodney, and Rodney looked at him. "I think of it this way: Every wrinkle on Rodney's face is a memory. We've been together so long I know those lines as well as I know my own. I remember how it was when we first met. Smooth skin, sometimes rough with stubble. Good jawline. Eyes crinkling when he smiled. And it just got better and better as the years went on. Lines around the mouth, the eyes, lines across the forehead. A map to our lives. You can see everything we've been through, all the highs and lows. It's etched into his face and mine."

Rodney smiled. A small thing, a quick upward tug of the lips, only for Don. He was like that. Not with everyone, but it could take time for him to warm up to people. And yet, here, so far from home and among strangers, that little smile. Their secret language.

Rodney looked at the young women and seemed to see a genuine willingness to listen. They didn't find that a lot these days, at least before the black hole came. *How like the youth*, Don thought to himself. *We were the exact same way.*

Rodney spoke about history. Not just his and Don's, but their community history. How many people thought the Stonewall riots were the start of the gay rights movement. Not so, he said. That was earlier in Silver Lake, California. A bar called the Black Cat. Still there, he said. Still has the same sign. Police raided the bar, as they did others. Queer people of all stripes were pissed, not wanting to take it anymore. They fought back. They were the first. He talked about how they went to Tucson, once. Just happened to be there for Pride. Did Becca and Amy know why Pride started in Tucson? No, they'd said, tell us. It was because a gay man named Richard Heakin—visiting from out of state—was murdered after he left a local gay bar. The culprits? Teenagers. Their punishment? Probation. Gays and lesbians said no, no, no. He told them of Matthew Shepherd, the young queer man left to die by people who hated his light. Amy had seen a play about him. He was the one they tied to a fence, she told Becca in a hushed voice. Did they know the harm Reagan caused? Did they have any idea of the effects that trickle-down economics had? Or how the Great Actor's war on drugs decimated Black communities without a care for the destruction left in the wake? Surely, Rodney said, they had to know about HIV, about AIDS, how Ol' Ronny ignored the cries, ignored people begging for help. Oh, and don't forget about Ms.

Nancy. Two poisoned people, he said. There's a reason Amy and Becca didn't see many people of old age in the queer community. So many were left to die, to be confined to a hospital, not allowed to be touched by anyone, lesions forming, skin stretching, stretching until they were pale skeletons. And still the Man in Charge did nothing. He did *nothing*. He refused to even acknowledge it.

Rodney said, "If there's a Hell, I know Ron and Nance are there. They are burning. They are suffering. They'll do so for eternity, and it still won't be enough. I don't care if everything goes with the eventual heat death of the entire universe, I hope they will still burn."

It wasn't a one-way conversation. Though they seemed to be hanging on Rodney's every word, Becca and Amy dotted his stories with little bursts of "Holy shit, that's crazy" and "Honestly, fuck all those people" and "Go, gays!"—that last shocking Rodney and Don into surprised laughter. Because they were young, they looked as if they wanted to roll their eyes every now and then, like when Rodney asked if they knew about HIV and AIDS, but they listened all the same.

Rodney said he might have been lost. Might have gone the way so many of their friends did. But he met Don. He met Don and knew that was it. But that didn't stop it from happening to people they knew, people they loved. Men like Nick, the first of their friend group to go. It was not slow. It was not easy. He screamed. No one could stop him from screaming. And then he died. The first, but not the last. Greg was next. Then Michael. Then Bobby and Ricky D and Joseph and the other Joseph and Miguel and Dwayne and Jerome and Paul and Timothy and Alan and Lonnie. He told them of the reason why it's LGBT when it used to be GLBT. It was an honor bestowed upon lesbians, who were some of the only people to stay with the dying men. They filled the hospitals, the streets, they cried out in horror at the treatment of the dying. "We put them first," Rodney said, "because they put us first. Never forget that. When we were abandoned by the world, it was the women from our community who held our hands as we passed."

Becca told them of a friend of theirs, a trans woman who had been physically and psychologically abused as a child, their gender in flux, yearning for their insides to match their outsides, her name—her *real* name—whispered under the blankets at night like a prayer. Simple, really: Anne. She loved the name Anne. Not Annie, not Ann with no *e*. Anne. And when she escaped, when she found freedom, she spoke the name aloud and that was who she was. That was who she'd always been. Then they'd watched as the courts had upheld bans on gender-affirming care, and wondered why so many people gave a shit about things that didn't affect them. "Like, who cares?" Amy groused. "A trans person living their true lives causes people thousands of miles away to melt down? It's crazy that we have to die the same way *they* do."

Rodney continued into the nineties, the Clintons. Don't ask, don't tell. Keep it a secret, they said. Stay hidden in the shadows. See all those straight couples? You don't get to be like them. You have to skulk around. You don't get to walk down the street in broad daylight holding hands. Straight couples? Sure, sure. But when it was same-sex? No, that was quite a step too far. But they didn't stay hidden. They didn't let people forget how many had died, how many were still dying. People were paying attention now. Not, of course, with enough time to save those lost. No. Besides, so many people thought, didn't they kind of deserve it? After all, maybe if they were normal like everyone else, it wouldn't have happened. Oh, what do you mean straight people can get it? Drug users. Yes, that's what it is. Gays and druggies. They should have made better choices.

Men in Charge, Rodney said, all of them, no matter what side of the aisle they're on, are all criminals. Every single one of them.

In a just world, anyone who was elected president would do so knowing that once their term was over, they'd go directly to prison for war crimes, no ifs, ands, or buts. Every single one of them. See how many Men in Charge would be keen on harming others if that were the case.

What made all of this so funny, Rodney said, was that he used to be conservative, at least fiscally. It took his people dying for him to see no one in power cared about anything other than themselves. After that, he washed his hands of all of it. He didn't give two shits about any of them. Some, he acknowledged, were worse than others, but in the end, liars and criminals, all.

They listened, Becca and Amy. When Don looked at them, they were enraptured by the low cadence of Rodney's voice. Some of his words were a bit more forceful, but overall, a calm, even tempo. He talked and talked, and they listened. And when they told him about what they'd seen, what they'd lived through, Rodney listened too. Stories of their history, of their community. Don wasn't sure when he'd last heard Rodney talk so much at once.

He wasn't surprised when a single tear fell from his eye. A thought had struck him dumb—profound in ways he didn't quite understand and might never have time to. How long had humans been gathering around a fire and sharing stories? Since the beginning, Don suspected. Since language was formed. Since words could be spoken. Sharing thoughts formed in the mind. Was it humankind's most singular achievement? Don thought it might be.

When Rodney finished, Amy and Becca both rose silently, almost as if they shared the same brain. They leaned over Rodney, Amy to his left, Becca to his right. They kissed his cheeks, once, Amy leaving a small imprint in pink.

"Thank you," Amy said. "Thank you for sharing yourself with us. I'll never forget it for as long as I live."

Becca sighed. "Amy, what the fuck."

Amy turned to her, eyes wide. "They should go with us."

Don startled. "Oh, hey, no, we have somewhere we need to—"

Becca shook her head. "She didn't mean it like that. We're staying here until it happens. No better place to be. We're going swimming. A night swim. Most of the people here go. We've done it every night over the past week."

"Isn't it cold?" Don asked with a frown. "That's melted glacier water."

"Cold as a witch's tit," Becca agreed cheerfully. "I would say you get used to it, but no, you really don't. I made it eight minutes last night. That's the longest I've gotten. Amy's gone ten. Some guy from Canada—name's . . . Dale? Dustin?—can stay out for hours. Don't know how he does it. Said it's because he's full of Tim Hortons."

"We don't have swimwear," Rodney said, and Don relaxed a little.

Until Becca and Amy exchanged a look. Amy smiled and said, "Yeah, see, that's the other thing."

The other thing, as it turned out, was that no one wore swimsuits. In fact, no one wore anything at all. Every person going into the water began to disrobe right there on the beach, leaving their clothes and undergarments folded in neat piles on the rocks and sand. Didn't matter the age; everyone who participated understood one had to be fully nude. The few who didn't swim stayed around a large bonfire, keeping it blazing for those fleeing frigid waters.

Don didn't think he'd seen so many exposed genitals since his days in New York in the early seventies. Back rooms, bathhouses, theaters that showed porn where the floor was sticky more often than not. The difference being that here, now, it felt strangely asexual. There was nothing erotic about the exposed flesh. There wasn't meant to be.

"They've lost their minds," Rodney said as the first people began to splash in the water, shrieking about how cold it was. The night above: few stars in a sky the color of old wood, the moon fat and bright orange as if on fire.

"Yes, they have," Don replied. He didn't think. He just acted. Reaching up and unbuttoning his shirt. The first, the second, the third, the fourth, the fifth, the sixth. Not cold, but borderline. His skin marbled, stomach, chest, arms as he slid off his shirt and let it fall to the ground.

He felt Rodney looking at him. "Seriously."

His trembling hands went to his pants, the button, the zipper.

Rodney said, "You will catch a *cold*."

Don laughed. "By the time it hits, we'll be gone." How wonderfully liberating that was! To act impulsively, to not worry about what could come. Why hadn't he done this more? Ah, wasn't that the rub.

He shoved down his pants and underpants in one smooth motion. No one looked at him aside from Rodney. No one cared. Leaning on Rodney's shoulder, he stepped out of his shoes, his socks, his pants and underpants. His bare feet touched sand. He breathed in as much as his lungs could take. His ribs creaked. He let it out. And then began to march toward the water, determined.

And he only made it two steps before a hand wrapped around his wrist. He turned, ready to snap at Rodney, to tell him he wanted to do this, that nothing could stop him, and that was that. He should have known better.

Rodney looked resigned. "Hold on a goddamn minute," he muttered. And then he began to undress.

How giddy that made Don. He thought that maybe love—a well-worn love, like a cherished old sweater—could still be exciting, surprising. Extraordinary, even. Was it sexual now, between them? Yes and no. Don admired Rodney's body as a lover, but it went beyond that. You love someone long enough, their bodies become comfort, a home in blood and bone. The scar from his bypass. The constellation of small moles on his left shoulder. The wiry gray-white hairs on his chest. Outie belly button. Lovely, soft skin, sagging slightly in the chest. Bony hips, pubic hair the same gray-white, skinny thighs, knobby knees. Long toes, especially on the right foot. Don hadn't lied when he'd told the women the lines and wrinkles were memories. He'd worshiped at the altar of Rodney for four decades. Beautiful, obstinate man. How breathless he made Don feel, even now. Even after all this time.

"You old fool," Rodney said fondly, knowing Don's thoughts like he always did. "Same as I always am. Busted but upright."

"Tonight," Don said. "When we go to bed, I think I'm going to ride you into that shitty mattress. Well, as much as my back will allow, anyway."

With that, he turned back to the water and marched toward it. If he put a little wiggle in his hips, well. That was for Rodney, and Rodney alone. And if the choked noise behind him meant anything, mission accomplished. He still had it, even after all these years.

The water was cold, and brutally so. It hurt, but in an almost indescribable way. Good pain, followed by encroaching numbness and the dulling of the mind. Don's head cleared when Rodney yelped from somewhere behind him. Don turned, up to his knees, not daring to go into the Forbidden Zone quite yet. Rodney was hopping from foot to foot, water splashing onto his bits and bobs. People cheered from farther into the lake. Don heard Amy shout, "Those are my queer elders! I love those guys!"

"I hate this," Rodney said as he stalked toward Don, water rising around him. "So, so much." But he did not stop when he reached Don. Instead, he continued on. The water rose to his thighs, then his upper thighs, and he yelled when it hit his crotch, but he kept on going. To his hips, to his stomach, to his chest. Before he sank underneath the water, he turned to Don and called, "I know you too. Everything there is to know. Come on, slowpoke. You and me have a date after this. I'm going to make you cross-eyed."

And then he sucked in a breath and went under.

Don didn't wait. Moving as fast as he could, ignoring the wild sensation against his penis and testicles, he awkwardly dove into the water a few feet away from where Rodney had disappeared maybe five, ten seconds before.

The shock was enormous, all-consuming. He couldn't think, mind a sheet of static. Time had no meaning. Flinched slightly when something brushed against his face. Relaxed against the fingers, the palms. He opened his eyes. It hurt, the cold biting, and he could only keep them open for a second or two at a time. But what he saw in those brief moments—Rodney before him, blinking, blinking the same way, bubbles sliding out of his nose and up, the water so clear they looked like they were floating—he felt down to his old bones. Beauty in a broken world. He was kissed, then, under the water. Frozen lips against frozen lips. Rodney's air, Don's air, all the same.

He felt Rodney smile against him.

They both kicked up off the rocky floor, up and up and up, bellowing at the night sky, the stars, the moon, the universe.

True to his word, Don loved on Rodney that night, slow and sure. Started with a massage, getting his muscles warm, rubbing in lotion. Music from the cassette player in the RV, the only tape they had: *Rumours*, Fleetwood Mac. No candles, but then they didn't need them. The weird color of the sky, the moon, cast enough light.

Rodney groaned in appreciation when Don rubbed his feet, his ankles, his calves. By the time Don reached his thighs, Rodney was more than up for the challenge. It was lovely, between them. Gone were the days when it was fast and hard. In bathrooms at parties. In a park if they were feeling daring. Frantic, as if they were addicted to each other and chasing that next hit. But like all things, that had changed into something quieter, something so much stronger. There was pain, brief though it was. Don sighed and Rodney gripped his hips, fingers dimpling the skin.

It lasted, this quiet moment. It went on and on, neither ready to let it end. They kissed and mumbled against each other's lips. Don thought they might have even dozed for a bit, but then Rodney would rock his hips and Don would moan into his shoulder.

The climax wasn't shattering for either of them. It wasn't an explosion of fireworks. Perhaps it was transcendent.

They slept curled around each other.

Amy and Becca knocked bright and early. Both looked flushed, eyes wide.

"What is it?" Don asked, Rodney's chin hooked over his shoulder.

Amy said, "Mars is gone. The moon is next, and then it's so long, thanks for all the fish."

CHAPTER 6

The radio no longer worked. It turned on, the dial lighting up as it always did, but there was nothing but static across the bandwidth. A brief moment on the AM radio side of things: "Clair de Lune," again, sounding far, far away, the piano like a ghost before it, too, faded away.

Their phones were useless. No internet. No connection. Even emergency calls didn't go through. Don looked at his phone, knowing it'd been years since their son had answered their calls, but something about the phones no longer working cemented it in ways he wasn't ready for.

Which made things that much more worrisome. They didn't know how long they had left. Days? Hours? According to the last report anyone heard—the morning Mars broke apart the day before—experts thought there was less than a week left. When the black hole came for the moon, it would all be over. Earth's time as the only known planet to support life was coming to a close.

It was when they crossed over from Idaho into Washington state that their situation took a turn for the unbelievable.

The afternoon sky was a swirling mass of every color. It was almost as if the atmosphere itself was on fire and burning in shades of pink and green and indigo. The sun was an unsettling shade of chartreuse. It seemed to be losing its circular shape, now somewhat blobby in the sky.

They were on a forestry road in eastern Washington, winding their way through lowlands of the Cascades. As near as they could tell, they still had almost two hundred miles left to travel. Don's screenshots of the map he'd taken a couple of weeks before helped, but not much. At the very least, it kept them from getting too lost, especially when there were no signs.

The RV turned a corner and came to an abrupt stop, dust billowing around the tires.

Don looked up from one of the screenshotted maps from his phone, glancing over at Rodney. "Why'd we stop?" he asked. "Do you need a break?"

Rodney didn't reply. He didn't turn his head to look at Don. Instead, he stared off to the side of the road into the trees, mouth agape.

Don followed his gaze and made a strangled noise when he saw what Rodney was looking at.

He didn't understand it at first. Flashes of light, bright white and blue, casting shadows along the ground. The thing looked amorphous, the edges constantly moving, sizzling and snapping as it arced off thin streaks of electricity. It hovered above the ground, moving at a slow pace through the trees off the side of the road.

Don couldn't speak. He'd heard of ball lightning before—a rare thing that only a handful of people had ever witnessed. It moved as if sentient, slow and sure, avoiding tree trunks, low-hanging limbs. If it made a sound, he couldn't hear it from inside the RV.

He opened the passenger door. Rodney cursed and struggled with his seat belt as Don stepped outside, lost in his head. He wasn't in the present, the *now*; instead, he was years and years in the past, memories rising unbidden.

He couldn't remember when, exactly. Sometime in the eighties. A toy was all the rage. A plasma ball, they called it. A glass sphere set up on a black stand. Sold at toy stores. In museums. In classrooms. The ball was filled with noble gases: xenon, neon, krypton. Turn it on, and the beams of light moved like wind through beach grass. Touch the glass, and the lights would form around your hand.

A voice in his head, bright, happy, forever young: *They brought one to school today! We all got to touch it. Can we get one for my room? Please? Please? Please?*

"Jeremy," Don whispered.

A hand around his wrist.

Don blinked rapidly. He stood in front of the RV. About twenty feet away, the ball lightning moved through the trees. He could hear it now, the pop and sizzle, and something else that sounded like the lumbering of an old machine. He looked down at the hand on his wrist.

"Are you out of your damn mind?" Rodney snapped. "You can't get close to it. We don't know what it could do."

"He wanted one," Don said. "Remember? Those funny little things. The plasma balls. He begged and begged and begged until we gave in. He was so excited for it. He barely talked about anything else." Don shook his head. "No, it was *all* he talked about. He needed it because it was different, it was interesting, it was *magic*. And so we took him to the mall. Bought it, even though it was ridiculously expensive. Took it home. Set it up. Turned it on, and the *look* in his eyes. I'd never seen anything like it before."

Rodney let his hand go. He looked off into the trees. "Lasted a week before he forgot all about it. I don't think he ever touched it again."

Yes and no. A lie, a small one, but a lie nonetheless. He *had* touched it one more time, years later. Picked it up, held it above his head, and then hurled it at the wall. The glass had shattered all over the floor. Later, when he was gone and the house was deathly silent, Don had sat on his knees, carefully picking up each piece of glass. Rodney knew this. Of course he did.

Close. So close. Too close, really, but that was the point of all of this, wasn't it? To see him again?

They looked off into the trees once more. The ball lightning continued to move at a slow pace, still as bright as ever. Even now, at the end of the world, an endless curiosity over such a thing. How? Why? He would never know the answer. It hurt more than he thought it would.

He took Rodney's hand in his own. "You all right?"

Rodney squeezed his hand but didn't look at him. "I'm trying. It's . . . I'm trying."

"I know. I can see that."

"It's not getting easier."

"I don't know that it's supposed to. We . . . I think we did our best."

Rodney glanced at him, eyes wide. "Even with . . ." He didn't finish. But then, he didn't need to. Don knew what he meant. He thought maybe they were as close as they'd ever been to accepting the truth. Not about the black hole, or the death of the planet. No, something that was at once both much bigger and much smaller than the universe.

"Even with," Don said firmly. "I know it doesn't feel like it, but we tried as much as we could. We did the best we could. But, sometimes your best still isn't good enough. And good lord, does it feel like failure."

Rodney didn't speak for a long while, looking out at the ball lightning as it moved through the trees. He wiped his eyes with the back of his hand. "He would have loved this. All of it. It would've set his imagination on fire."

"I know," Don whispered.

It was almost time.

Rodney said, "Do you feel that?"

"What?"

"I don't know. I feel . . . lighter, somehow. My back doesn't hurt as much as it did before. Shoulders and neck too. They feel better than they have in years." He huffed out an amused breath. "Not that it'll matter for long."

Don paused, turning inward. He hadn't noticed it before when he'd stepped out of the truck, too distracted by the ball lightning. Rodney was right: He *did* feel lighter. Not as if the weight of all of life had suddenly lifted from his shoulders, but something close to it. For a moment, he felt younger than he had in years, all the earthly aches and pains seemingly melting away.

"Strange," Don murmured.

It seemed as if the universe itself wasn't done fucking with Rodney and Don. They took it slow down the roads, keeping an eye out for more weird things that they could not explain. As they continued on, that feeling of lightness only intensified. Don wondered what it would feel like to just . . . float away.

Hours left in their trip. Mere hours. So close Don could almost taste it. He did not look at the precious box sitting back on the shelf. He didn't need to. He knew it was still there, safe and sound. Their surroundings weren't yet familiar, but with any luck, they soon would be.

But then, near twilight, the RV began to shudder and shake. Smoke streamed from underneath the hood, filling the interior of the RV with a noxious stench. Rodney pulled off to the side of the road. The engine growled and snarled. Then it hitched once, twice, three times. A moment later, it died a groaning death, clicking and ticking until there was nothing but silence.

Rodney turned the key to the off position. Waited a moment. Tried to start the RV. The engine chugged but didn't catch. He tried again. And again. And again. By the last time he tried, the engine didn't make a sound.

"Gas?" Don asked, knowing that wasn't the case.

Rodney shook his head in frustration. "Still have half a tank. It's not that."

"It's the black hole."

"Or we bought a shitty, decades-old RV that finally gave up the ghost." Rodney scrubbed a hand over his face. "I don't know. It feels like I don't know anything anymore." Without another word, he opened the door and got out. He moved around to the front of the RV and lifted the hood. More smoke bloomed upward and outward, Rodney waving his hand through it to try and make it dissipate. Don heard him digging around, cursing underneath his breath.

He was out there for a good fifteen minutes before he slammed the hood down. Looking at Don through the windshield, he shook his head. He looked exhausted.

Don got out of the RV and joined Rodney at the front. He was surprised when it felt like his foot took longer than it should have done to reach the ground. When he stood, he stretched, arms over his head. His back popped in ways it hadn't since he was in his fifties, not young, but not quite old, either. He didn't know why, but physically, he felt right as rain. The same couldn't be said for the RV. "It's dead?"

Rodney's hands were balled into fists at his sides. "Think so. Even if I knew how to fix it, I don't have any tools."

Don gripped Rodney's elbow, comfort for them both. "We still have a ways to go."

Rodney hung his head. "Even if we started walking, we wouldn't make it in time. I don't even know what the nearest town is."

"Brief, Washington," Don said. "It's a ghost town. Nothing there."

"And the tower is . . . what. A hundred miles away?"

"A little over, yes."

Rodney jerked his arm out of Don's grip, spinning around. He slammed his hands on the hood of the RV over and over, teeth bared. Don could handle this. He'd rather Rodney be angry than dead in the eyes and heart like Amelia. He wondered where she was, what she was doing. Was she even still alive, or did she take Rodney's advice and go to the barn herself? After all, she'd had two bullets left, or so she'd said.

Don let his husband have his anger, his rage. It would be unfair to try and take that from him. All of this was unfair. Every bit of it. They were close, so close, and *this* was how it ended? In failure. On the side of a forgotten road in Washington. Maybe if they'd gone faster. Maybe if they hadn't stopped as much as they had, allowed themselves to become distracted by people. Good people. Bad people. All diversions, and for what? Yes, they'd seen little pockets of humanity, but what about what *they* wanted? What about the reason they'd undertaken this journey in the first place?

"He wouldn't blame us," Don finally said. "Not because of this. We tried."

Rodney scoffed. "Did we? Because it sure as shit feels like we waited until the end of the world to get our asses in gear. We could have done this last year. Or the year before. But no. We waited and waited and waited until we didn't have a choice."

"We're here, aren't we? Because we chose to be."

"And it's still not good enough. We've come up short, once again. Aren't you tired of that feeling? That, no matter what you do, it won't change a goddamn thing?" Spat out through gritted teeth. Not angry with Don, just . . . angry.

Don said, "We just need to think. There must be a house around here. Multiple houses. If we can find one, we can find a car. And if we can find a car, we can make it. I know we can. It'll take time we don't have but we have to try."

"It's weird," Rodney said, tilting his head back toward the sky. "I'm tired. Exhausted, really. Not a normal tired, either. It's in my bones."

"But," Don said, knowing there was more.

"But," Rodney said, "I . . . I don't know. I feel . . . almost weightless. Like I'm here, but I have no heft to me."

"You feel younger," Don said.

Rodney looked at him, surprised. "How did you . . . ?"

"I do too," Don said. He reached up and touched his face. Still the same shape: soft, lined with wrinkles. "I don't feel like I look."

"You look fine."

"Thank you, dear. But that's not what I meant."

"We're too old for this shit."

"Probably."

"And yet, here we are."

"Here we are," Don agreed, kissing his cheek.

Rodney said, "I didn't know what would happen when we first met. I didn't know that it'd be a lifetime. I hoped it would, I think. At least part of me did. I couldn't even tell you why. But there was something about you, something I wanted. Something I thought I needed. And I was right. I *did* need you. Still do, in fact."

"How lucky are we?" Don asked.

Rodney snorted as he stood upright, turning to face his husband. "How do you figure?"

"You said that that's what the universe is. Luck and happenstance. There's no fate, no destiny. Sometimes it is horrible, devastating. But sometimes, it could lead to a life we couldn't have predicted. A good life, even if it hurts. Out of everything in the universe, what were the chances that we'd find each other the way we did?"

"One in a trillion."

"Probably not quite that high, but it might as well have been. If it was luck that brought us together, then I think we're the luckiest people in the world."

"Even now?" Rodney asked, eyebrows rising up his forehead.

"Even now."

"That's—"

"A truck," Rodney said, eyes going wide.

Don frowned. "What?"

"A *truck*," Rodney said again, grabbing Don by the chin and turning his head. Sure enough, a small truck was driving up the road toward them. A little Nissan, from the late eighties or early nineties by the look of it. Faded blue with a spotlight sitting above the driver's-side mirror. Ever the protector, Rodney stepped in front of Don, stance wide, arms across his chest. Even at the end of the world, his machismo knew no bounds. What a lovely asshole he was.

The truck stopped about ten feet away from them, the headlights remaining on. Don couldn't make out who was inside; the dusty headlights were a tad too bright. A driver behind the wheel, and someone—something?—in the passenger seat. The spotlight turned on, shining directly at them. They flinched, raising their hands to block their eyes.

Don thought of Amy. Of Becca. The family. Pantomime. Amelia. Who would this person prove to be?

The truck turned off. The door opened.

The woman who stepped out seemed as tall as she was wide. Taller than both Rodney and Don; it was almost impossible how much of her there was stepping outside the small truck. She looked to be in her forties or fifties, face slightly weathered, dark brown skin, with tight braids against her scalp. She wore baggy khakis with multiple pockets, a vest over a plaid shirt, and dusty boots. She whistled once, a sharp burst. A large black-and-brown dog jumped out after her. A German shepherd mix of some kind, and a beautiful one at that, its coat shiny. Its pointy ears turned toward them as it got its feet under it, tongue lolling. Around its middle, a vest of sorts, orange with bulky pockets that looked packed tightly.

The woman raised a hand, cautious. “Hello there, folks. Some car trouble? Thought that might be the case. Saw your headlights from my porch up a ways.” She threw a thumb over her shoulder. “Thought maybe you could use some help.”

“You live out here?” Rodney asked.

“Sure do. Far enough away from everything that I can hear myself think, but not so much that I can’t get supplies when I need them. Have a cabin about half a mile up.” The dog sat at her side, head on a swivel.

“Our RV broke down,” Don said. “We’re trying to get to Copper Mountain.”

The woman whistled, the dog’s ears twitching. “That’s not close. Still got about a hundred and twenty miles to go. Tell you what: If you’d like, I can take a look under the hood. Pretty handy, if I do say so myself. Can’t make any promises, but I can try.”

“Everything is broken,” Don said stupidly.

“It is,” the woman agreed. “Gravity, too, I think.”

“What?” Rodney asked, as he and Don exchanged a glance.

“You don’t feel it? Something changed. I saw rocks floating along the road on the way down here. And when I jumped off the porch, it took me a couple of seconds longer than it should have to reach the ground.”

“That’s why . . .” Don glanced at Rodney, who nodded but didn’t speak.

The woman watched them curiously. “Yeah, you feel it too, don’t you.” Not a question. Then, “I’ll be honest, though. I’m more concerned about the sky. It’s not supposed to look like that.” She shook her head. “Name’s Jerri. Dog is Naks. Good girl. She’ll probably sniff your crotches, so have fun with that. Had to put a weighted vest on her this morning. Didn't want her to accidentally fly away."

The dog's tongue lolled out of her mouth happily, as if flying away sounded like a grand old time.

Jerri clapped her hands and said, "Okay! Why don't you tell me about yourselves while I see what's what?"

It didn't take her long to say there was nothing she could do. "See that?" Jerri said, pointing at some part of the engine that Don had no idea about. It all looked the same to him. "Rusted, broken off. You'd need to get it replaced if you want it to start again."

"Can you fix it?" Rodney asked.

"Nope. And even if I could, there wouldn't be enough time. Take at least a week. Nah, this is where she stays." She patted the grille. "Final resting place for the old girl. And she'll have a front-row seat to whatever happens. A good way to go."

Don sank to the road, face in his hands. "It can't end like this. It just can't."

"Oh, hey," Jerri said. "I'm sorry I can't do more. That's a tough break."

Don dropped his hands when he heard the RV door open. Standing with a groan, he looked through the windshield. Rodney was inside, moving between the seats to the rear of the RV. Naks sat on the road next to Jerri, both watching the RV.

"What's he doing?" Jerri asked.

"I have no idea," Don said with a sigh.

A few minutes later, Rodney climbed back out of the RV. He carried two backpacks: his and Don's. After closing the RV door, he leaned his head against it. "You got us this far," Don heard him say. "More than I expected. Appreciate that. Sorry it had to end like this." With that done, he marched to the front of the RV once more, looking determined. Handing Don his backpack, he said, "If we're going to go, we need to go now."

"You want to walk the rest of the way?" Jerri asked, aghast. "That's impossible. You'll never make it in time."

Don shouldered his backpack. "Have to try. We made a promise." Speaking of. "Where is—"

"Safe," Rodney said. "I got him."

Don nodded. An hour before, and he would have said his knees weren't looking forward to the road ahead. But now, with this lightness about them, he thought maybe, just maybe, they'd have a chance. A fool's notion, to be sure, but it was either that or give up here and now. And that wasn't an option.

Jerri said, "God*damn*, I like you guys. You're crazy. Most people don't like to show strangers their crazy, but here you both are, letting it all hang out. Good for you."

"It was nice to meet you," Don said. "Thank you for stopping to help us."

They'd almost made it to her truck when she called from behind them. "So, Naks has an idea."

Don stopped and looked over his shoulder. "Naks? The dog?"

Jerri shrugged as Naks panted, head cocked. "I didn't say it was a *good* idea, but yeah."

"You hear that?" Don asked Rodney. "The dog has an idea."

"I bet it does," Rodney muttered. Raising his voice, he said, "What's the idea?"

"I want to show you something," Jerri said. "I need another person to see it to make sure I'm not losing my mind." She laughed. "Any more than I already have. In exchange, I'll give you my truck."

Don blinked. "What? We can't take your—"

"I'm not going to need it," she said. "Come what may, I'm fine right where I am. But you folks aren't." She pointed back up the road. "My cabin isn't far. Won't take long, and you can be on your way."

Rodney said, "What do you want to show us?"

She shrugged. "If I told you, you wouldn't believe me."

True to Jerri's word, they didn't have to go far. Five minutes up the road, she turned the truck down a small driveway hidden by overgrown trees and shrubs. Almost full-on dark. Branches scraped the sides of the truck, causing Don to wince. Naks sniffed Rodney's crotch thoroughly just as Jerri said she would. Rodney suffered in silence.

Until Jerri pointed out the rocks captured in the truck's headlights. Not all of them. Small pebbles, really, but they were floating a few inches above the ground. Then Jerri said, "Look at the trees."

Pine trees. Conifers. And their branches didn't sway side to side. Instead, it looked as if the limbs were *rising*, like one of those fake Christmas trees that had been boxed away, the wire branches sticking straight up. It was as if the trees were reaching toward the sky.

"How long has it been like this?" Rodney asked.

"Since last night," Jerri said. "This morning, I saw a squirrel try to leap from one tree to another. It . . . just kept floating. Didn't see where it landed." Under her breath, she added, "If it did."

The truck crested a small hill, and there, set back against a grove of trees, a small log cabin, the roof made of dark green metal. Underneath the front windows, wooden boxes that held soil and flowers in yellow and pink and purple. A small porch with a rocking chair next to a dog bed that looked as if it'd been chewed on a few times.

Don stepped out of the truck onto gravel and froze when he saw light moving through the trees about a quarter of a mile away.

Behind him, Rodney said, "What are you doing?"

"Did it follow us?" Don asked in a hushed voice.

Rodney climbed out of the truck, following Don's gaze. "What on earth . . . ?"

"Ball lightning," Jerri said, appearing beside them, causing them both to jump. "Very rare. I've only seen it once before, when I was a kid. It's been like this almost every night for the past week. It sticks around for an hour or two and then just . . . vanishes."

"We saw it earlier," Don said. "Before you showed up. It's why we stopped. What . . . *why* is it?"

Jerri shrugged. "I don't question things anymore. For all I know, it's the Earth's response to what's coming. It never comes any closer than it is right now. I'm not worried about it. I'm worried about the moon."

"What about it?" Don asked, looking up. He saw what she meant. He didn't know how else to think of it but this: The moon now looked like a comet. Something was happening on the surface of the moon, something that caused a streak of white to trail off to one side of it, as if all the dirt and dust and rock on the surface was getting pulled into space. "Oh my god."

"Yeah," Jerri said in a low voice. "I don't know how much longer she can hold on."

She didn't invite them inside; rather, she led them to the side of the house, Naks bringing up the rear, tail wagging furiously. In front of them, hills and rolling fields as far as the eye could see. Tall grasses swayed. Trees reached toward the oddly colored sky.

"What are we looking for?" Don asked.

"Give it a minute," she said without looking at them. "What's at Copper Mountain?"

"A promise we need to keep," Don said.

"A serious promise?"

"Yes," Rodney said.

Jerri nodded. "I get that. I've made those kinds of promises before. To others. To myself. But I didn't keep some of them. Maybe a lot of them."

"Why?" Don asked, despite himself.

"Because sometimes, the people asking for the promise didn't have my best interests in mind. People can be cruel, selfish, only thinking about themselves even as they inflict harm on others."

"Is that why you moved out here?" Rodney asked.

"Partly," Jerri said, still looking out at the moonlit fields. "I don't have to answer to anyone but myself. I spent years trying to be something I'm not, and I had to make a decision: Either I got out, or I stayed and nothing changed." She laughed to herself. "Hardly anyone out here looks like me, but fuck it. I got out of a bad situation, and I sought absolution. I don't think I could have asked for a better place to find it."

"Did you?" Don asked, thinking of a great many things.

"Maybe, maybe not. But it's enough for me." She glanced at them. "Absolution. You want to know what I learned about it?"

Rodney nodded.

"You have to want it. Above all else. Because it's *so easy* to stay stuck down in the muck. Even as it tears at you, it feels safe because it's familiar. But that safety is a lie. The muck is filled with apathy that can spread like poison."

"It's not that easy," Rodney said.

"But it doesn't have to be as hard as people make it out to be," Jerri said. "Easier said than done, I know, but you can't hold on to everything all the time."

Don said, "We can try."

She grinned at them. "Even now? Even near the end?" Glancing down at her watch, she said, "It's almost time."

"For what?" Rodney asked as Naks sniffed his trousers.

Jerri said, "I'm not a big people person. Never really have been. Humans made art and music and dancing and books and films.

People just . . . continually disappoint. For all the cool things that exist, there are people trying to take it all away. It's why I like animals. A dog doesn't give two shits if you think you're a failure. To them, you're their entire world. Isn't that crazy? To us, dogs are part of our world. They come, and if we're lucky, stick around for a good long time. And then they leave us, bereft but so thankful we had the time we did. But to dogs, we're their *entire* world." She reached down and gave Naks a good scratch around her ears. "Have you thought about the animals?"

Don blinked, looking at Rodney. "The animals?"

Jerri nodded. "The whales, the giraffes. The insects and the birds who eat them. Dogs, cats. Walruses. Lions. Wolves. Muskrats. Living in ignorance about what's coming. They'll know, before the end, but not like we have. They haven't spent the last year holding their breaths, wondering what news is going to be given today. They know this earth just the same as we do. Maybe even better. It's said ignorance is bliss. We know that's not true, even though we're animals. It's more of a blissful unawareness. Isn't that a gnarly way to live? I wish I could have been an animal. I always wanted to be, ever since I could remember. They're not so different than us. Wilder, more feral, but they have minds all the same. I respect them, on their terms. I never force myself. That's the problem with people. We insist. We call it persistence, but it's all so selfish. All to protect our own interests."

"Don't animals do the same?" Rodney asked.

"No," Jerri said. "There's a difference. They run on instinct, on survival. We think we're smarter, we think we know more, that we're better in every regard, only to show our whole asses by stealing land or taking our weapons to other countries and using American-made bombs to spread the message of freedom through exceptionalism. We're territorial, and greedy. That land is rich, why can't I have it? Those people have something I don't, and I want it. I'll take it from them. Look at that land, I should own it. See those mountains? Those trees? The rolling hills? It belongs to someone or something else, but why can't *I* take it?"

"You sound as if you think humanity doesn't deserve to survive," Rodney said.

She waved him off. "That's not for me to decide. But don't act like there's an abundance of evidence to the contrary. We are an angry, violent species. Of course it was going to end this way. From fire we're made, and from fire we'll be unmade."

"Then what's the point of doing anything?" Don asked helplessly.

"Good question," Jerri said. "And one I don't know that I'll ever have an answer to. Do you know?"

Don shook his head, dumbfounded.

Jerri sighed. "I'm not trying to—" Then, "It's starting. Like clockwork." She turned back toward the fields.

Don and Rodney did too. Beyond them, open land. Mountains in the distance. Trees reaching toward the heavens. Flashes of light: ball lightning floating above the ground, though too far away to be dangerous. But all that fell away when he saw what Jerri was trying to show them.

At first, his mind couldn't compute what he was seeing coming from the trees. It felt like a fever dream.

Animals. Dozens and dozens of animals. Deer, both does and bucks. Elk, their hair thick around their necks and chests. At least ten mountain goats, their bodies white and muscular, black horns protruding from their heads. Squirrels. Chipmunks. Coyotes. Cougars. A trio of black bears, one larger than the other two. Cattle. Horses. Lizards. Snakes. Voles. Varieties of birds flying above them, some tiny, some with wingspans of at least ten feet, all flying awkwardly, almost floating, as if they too felt the change in gravity. As the people watched, the animals began to walk in a wide circle. It was only then Don saw similar circles in the fields around the house.

"It started a week ago," Jerri said as the animals moved slowly. "First, it was just deer. Same time every night. They'd appear, walk in a circle for a while, and then disappear. Three days ago, the birds came with them. Two days ago, the elk, the goats, the wild horses. The bears are new. Haven't seen them before. I wondered if the predators would only see prey, but so far, that hasn't been the case."

"What are they doing?" Rodney whispered.

"They know," Jerri said. "They might not know *what* they know, but they know something." She sniffled, wiping her eyes with the back of her hand. "What do you think humanity's legacy will be?"

"Why does it matter?" Rodney asked. "There won't be anyone left to remember it."

"*Rodney*," Don said, mortified. "You can't just—"

"He's right," Jerri said, clear-eyed. "It'll all be gone. No one will remember what we did here. No one will remember all the good and terrible things people did." She laughed.

"Do we live to be remembered?" Don asked. "Or do we live to live?"

"Is there a difference in the end?" Jerri asked.

"We're not all bad," Rodney said.

"Of course not," Jerri said. "But those of us who are tend to be the loudest. And much of the rest choose to ignore them, pretending they don't exist. They want to believe we're part of some exceptional utopia rather than reality. No, our legacy—if that's what it can be called—is a lie. Humanity grew through the destruction of others, of the land, the animals, the people. Sometimes, I wonder if we're the disease, and this is just the universe's way of inoculating against further infection. It's the only way I can rationalize this."

Don hadn't thought much of the idea of legacy in a long time. Any and all hope for such things had fallen apart a decade before, when the phone had rung on a winter afternoon. He hated how much he'd been expecting that call. For years, he wondered every time he picked up the phone if *this* was going to be the news they'd been dreading, the news that felt like it was inevitable. It never was until it was.

"I don't know that we deserve to be remembered," Jerri said. "But then there's a part of me, a big part, a human part, that says I'm wrong. That even with all our faults, we did something special. We were something extraordinary. Of all the chances in the universe, what's the likelihood that we'd have survived long enough to learn to love and hate? It's minuscule. Of course it is. If it wasn't, we'd have found others long ago. And now, another minuscule chance has happened."

"One in a trillion," Rodney murmured.

"Exactly," Jerri said, startling them both when she clapped her hands.

"Luck," Don said. "Rotten, shitty luck."

Jerri laughed. "It is. So much. But here we are, strangers who never would have met. Maybe that's what the point of all of this was. To have these random moments of collision, to learn from each other, to hear stories."

"To live," Rodney said.

Jerri looked back out at the animals. "I suppose you're right. And you gotta admit, the universe is hysterically funny. Why the hell else would I stumble upon two random white men at the end? Maybe it means something. Or maybe it means nothing at all. I think . . . I think I'm okay with that." Then she frowned. "Huh. That's never happened before."

Don and Rodney looked back out to the field. The animals had stopped moving. They still stood in a circle—at least a hundred of them in all—but they didn't move. Even the birds had landed. A fat crow stood on the horns of one of the elk.

Every single animal had their face turned up toward the sky.

"It's coming," Jerri said. "For better or worse, it's coming." She turned to look at them with dark eyes. Behind her, the animals stood stock-still, staring up at the moon. "We should get you two on the road."

She gave them her truck, saying again she no longer had need of it. She had what she wanted: a roof over her head, and Naks by her side.

"You could go with us," Don said. There wouldn't be much room, but he didn't like the idea of leaving her behind without a vehicle.

"Nah," she told them. "I'm where I'm supposed to be. We'll wait here."

She loaded them up with supplies, enough to last for a few days. No one said that there wouldn't be *anything* in a few days, but they didn't need to. They knew. Water, dried meat, fruit. She even put five cinder blocks in the bed of the truck. "Just in case gravity decides to play a few more tricks. Should keep you grounded. Though, I suppose if the whole truck starts to float, it won't matter much."

By then, it was nearing midnight, and though neither of them liked to drive at night, they were past such things now. Either they'd get on the road now, or they never would.

As they stood in front of the truck, Jerri said, "In movies, black holes sometimes lead to other places. A rip in space and time, sending you from one corner of the universe to another. Maybe that's what'll happen to us. Maybe we'll float away and when we wake up, everything will be the same, but different. A new sun, maybe blue. Constellations we've never seen before. I think that would be amazing."

"Thank you," Rodney said, taking her hand in his. "Thank you for helping us. You didn't have to."

She squeezed his hand as she chuckled. "I know I didn't. But everyone needs help, sometimes. Careful with the truck. Keep it below sixty if you can. She doesn't like going faster than that." Then she moved to Don. She stood in front of him for a moment, studying him. Then, "What's at Copper Mountain?"

Don said, "Absolution."

She nodded. "You might not make it all the way in the truck. Careful of the snowpack. Snow in the Cascades is like cement. You have a map?"

"We do," Don said.

She leaned forward and kissed him on the cheek before stepping back. "I hope you find what you're looking for. It must be something important."

"It is," Rodney said. "More than you know."

Jerri smiled at them. "Then I wish you all the best."

They drove down the driveway. In the side mirror, Don saw Jerri waving, Naks sitting beside her. He thrust his arm out the window and waved back.

Rodney pointed the truck west.

CHAPTER 7

Sixty miles to go. The sky looked like it was on fire. Two in the morning, and it was an odd sort of bright: almost like a full moon, but more powerful. Shadows danced along the roadway, the trees black shapes rising on either side of them, along with pebbles and pinecones, all hovering a few inches above the ground.

Slow going. Not only was it early (late?), but the ever-winding road continued to rise in elevation. Sometimes there were guardrails. Other times, none, with a sheer drop off that would certainly mean their deaths if the Nissan slipped over.

Rodney's hands gripped the steering wheel as he leaned forward, squinting at the road ahead. Don was on map duty once more, guiding him through as best he could using the screenshots he'd taken. So far, so good.

Ball lightning chased after them through the trees, bouncing up and down, leaving scorch marks against tree trunks and grass. Other lights, too, lights Don couldn't place. Little flashes of light bursting out of the ground in the tree line, then disappearing. Don wondered if it was the Earth crying out.

He said, "We're going to make it."

Rodney didn't say anything.

Don said, "We have time. We're on the right road. It's only a couple of hours more."

Rodney squeezed the steering wheel.

Don said, "Hopefully, the watchtower isn't—"

"I loved him," Rodney said. "With everything I had. More than I've loved anything. But, toward the end, I think I hated him too."

Don froze. He waited.

It did not take long. "I hated him," Rodney repeated, rigid in his seat. "For what he did. I didn't want to, but I did. It came out of nowhere. It was like a switch had flipped. I was sad and then it was like my insides had been replaced by molten steel. Like I was burning from the inside out. I felt it in my stomach. My heart. My lungs. I could barely breathe around it. I hated him, Don. For not trying. For not listening to us, even though it was so hard for him. Didn't he see that we wanted what was best for him? Didn't he see that we gave him every part of ourselves?" He slapped the steering wheel. "And for what? Where did it get us? What am I that I can even *think* something like that?"

Don looked away, throat bobbing up and down. He thought about the people they'd met on their journey west: the beauty, the ugliness. For every Becca and Amy and Jerri, there was an Amelia. There was a family wearing masks. He said, "You're human. Painfully, wonderfully human. I can't, and won't, blame you for feeling that way." He rubbed his sweat-slick palms against his thighs. "Especially when I felt the same way."

Rodney looked relieved. "I . . . I didn't want to. I tried everything I could to stop it. But it just kept growing and growing until I couldn't control it anymore. It'd been festering, I think. Festering for a long time. And then it just broke open, and all the poison spilled out into me. I couldn't stop it. Couldn't do anything but let it wash over me. And I remember thinking, no, no, this isn't how it should be. This isn't fair. Why do other people get to be happy but I don't?

Why do others get to live normal lives but I don't? Why did *this* happen to me? Selfish. So selfish. I didn't think about him. I didn't think about you. I was thinking about *me*. How it made me feel. How sad. How furious."

"You never said anything like this before."

"How could I?" Rodney asked. "How could I look you in the eyes and tell you that as much as I loved and hated him in equal measure, I hated myself even more? I couldn't stand to see the hurt on you, especially knowing I'd been the cause."

"So you chose to protect me from yourself."

"I suppose I did. I guess that—"

"As if you had the right."

Rodney's jaw tensed.

But Don didn't care. "As if you had the goddamn *right*," he snapped, anger bubbling in his chest. "As if I wasn't feeling the same way. As if I wasn't capable of handling whatever you had to throw at me. You weren't alone, Rodney. You weren't then, you aren't now. I love you. God knows I do. But sometimes, oh *sometimes*, you act like you're the only person in the world capable of dealing with pain. You act like if you take it all in on yourself, no one else will have to deal with it. Guess what? We do. *I* do. It leaked from you, your poison. I could smell it. Taste it, bitter and cold. How do you think that made me feel? But you weren't thinking of me. You said so yourself."

"It wasn't about you."

Wrong thing to say. "Bullshit. It was about *both* of us. Not just you. Not just me. Together. We were still here. We were and are still alive."

"For now," Rodney muttered as they rounded a corner. Ahead, the road stretched out before them. No other cars, just the headlights on the blacktop. Above, the cracked moon in a kaleidoscope sky.

"Don't give me that," Don retorted. "Who the hell do you think you are?"

"I'm your husband."

"Then maybe it's time you start acting like a partner."

Stricken, Rodney said, "You don't think I have been?"

"I think you got lost. To be fair, we both did. I wandered the house for days and weeks, sure that at any moment, he was going to burst in through the door. Maybe he'd be seven years old. Maybe he'd be an adult. But he'd come home and we would help him." A tear slipped down his cheek. "And he'd *want* our help. Unlike any other time before, he'd want it. But that didn't happen. So like you, I got lost. Without a map, without a guide. We were in the middle of a jungle and didn't know which way was out. Hell, maybe there wasn't a way out. Maybe we're still trapped there, and this is all just an illusion."

"You're real," Rodney said fiercely. "I am too. Somehow, we're still here."

They went quiet for a time, Don lost in memory, Rodney undoubtedly the same. Don had words lodged in his throat, words he needed to get out, but they were stuck. He swallowed once, twice. Then, in a quiet voice, he said, "I miss him."

Rodney sniffled. "I do too. Every day."

"Where do you think he is?"

"I don't know," Rodney said. "Nowhere. Everywhere. Maybe he's sitting in the truck with us. Maybe he's been with us the whole time. In Maine. On the road. Seeing all the things we've seen. The people. The places."

"He'd have loved it," Don said, looking out the window. "All of it. Even the scary parts."

"Especially the scary parts."

Don chuckled. Then laughed louder and louder. Before long,

Rodney joined in and under a dying sky, they laughed until they could barely breathe.

The ranger station was just as they'd remembered: a small, squat building in chocolate brown. A similar brown sign with yellow lettering let them know they were at the Copper Ridge trailhead. The lights were off in the building, no other cars in the parking lot, aside from an abandoned snowplow leaking salt out of its rear container.

Rodney pulled the truck into the parking lot, stopping parallel with the ranger station. Dawn was breaking, the sky taking on an orange-reddish hue, angry and bright. Shadows stretched long from the surrounding trees.

They didn't get out right away. Because all around them, things were floating. Pinecones. Rocks. Clumps of dirt. Leaves. Above the branches reaching toward the sky, a flock of birds. Some of them looked like they were flying upside down.

Don moved first, opening his door and stepping outside. It took a noticeable extra second or two for his feet to reach the ground. That feeling of lightness, of near weightlessness was stronger than it'd been at Jerri's cabin. Don wondered—just for a moment—what would happen if he jumped. Would he rise into the sky? Would he keep on going until he could see the curve of the Earth? It didn't scare him as much as he expected.

Don heard the driver's door open, and Rodney's grunt of surprise when he stepped out of the truck. Don looked over the hood at his husband. Rodney was staring down at his feet, forehead bunched up.

"I know," Don said.

Rodney lifted his head. "It's not supposed to be like this. I'm not supposed to feel good." He lifted his arms above his head.

Even from the other side of the truck, Don could hear Rodney's back crack, a quick *pop pop pop*. There was a smoothness to his face that hadn't been there the day before, as if the wrinkles around his eyes, his mouth, his forehead were all receding. It wasn't like Rodney suddenly appeared decades younger, but it wasn't *not* that, either. Perhaps not decades, but a good ten years younger? Sure. That wasn't outside the realm of possibility.

And that was to say nothing about Don himself. He could still feel his body. His arms, his legs. His chest and hips, his head upon his shoulders. But the crushing weight of living seemed to be lifting from his shoulders, as if the albatross around his neck had gotten tired of waiting in deepening misery. He didn't feel *better*, not exactly. And yet, watching a pinecone spin in midair off the side of the road was a sight he never expected to see, filling him with wonder.

Rodney rounded the front of the truck, their backpacks in hand. "He's in your bag. Safe."

Don nodded and took the bag from Rodney, gently, carefully, as if he held the most precious thing in the world. Which, of course, he did. He slung it over his shoulders. They were here. They had kept their promise.

"I recognize this place," Don said. "Didn't think I'd remember it as well as I do. There was that . . . guy? The forest ranger. Remember him? With the eyebrows."

Rodney snorted. "Yeah, I remember him. Thought he'd never shut up."

"He liked to talk, didn't he?"

"About anything and everything."

"Told that joke, too. How did it go?"

Rodney said, "Beautiful day in the forest. Park ranger gives warning about bears. Says brown bears are usually harmless. They avoid contact with humans, so it's suggested that campers and hikers tie small bells to their bags. They make noise and give the bears time to get out of the way. However, he said, *grizzly* bears are extremely dangerous. If you see any droppings from a grizzly, leave immediately."

Don played his part. "How do we know if they're grizzly bear droppings?"

Rodney looked at him, deadpan. "It's easy. They're full of small bells."

A beat of silence.

And then Rodney's lips twitched, mirth-filled eyes crinkling around the edges, that thing he did when he was trying not to laugh. Don didn't have that problem. It was a terrible joke, even after all these years, but that didn't matter. Don laughed. Rodney laughed too. They clung to each other as the laughter gave way to tears. Don didn't know who sobbed first. It didn't matter. It hit them both almost at the same time, and they cried. They cried until their lungs burned, until their faces felt like plastic. They cried until they saw their tears lifting from their faces, floating around them, glittering like tiny little stars. And then they laughed once more.

When they finished, Rodney kissed the side of Don's head and said, "Come on. We're almost there."

The trail should have been more difficult than it was. They were old men attempting to quickly climb a mountain, after all. But as they climbed higher and higher, no stitches formed in their sides. They were short of breath, but it was manageable. Beads of sweat dotted their brows (sometimes floating away like their tears), but they did not slow, they did not falter. Every now and then, they needed to push floating rocks out of the way. Partway up, a boulder the size of a dog spun in front of them, blocking the path. Don and Rodney pushed it out of the way. It went over the edge with ease, but it didn't fall. It hung suspended, spinning slowly.

They caught glimpses of the lookout tower from a distance, the top of the structure sticking out from among the waving branches of tall fir trees. It still stood. Don didn't know what he would've done if it had been gone. They hadn't been here in over thirty years. So many things could have changed.

They were still a quarter of a mile away when the light suddenly shifted. Not quite day-bright, but close; and then it was as if the world had been plunged into darkness. They both froze. A small waterfall ran down the rock face, gurgling.

"What happened?" Don asked, heart in his throat. "Is it—"

"The moon," Rodney said, staring up at the sky.

Don looked up and gasped, hands shaking. The moon had split, breaking into huge chunks surrounded by a gigantic cloud of dust. It didn't seem real.

"We're running out of time," Don whispered.

And then the ground began to shake under their feet. Don looked back the way they'd come. A bright flash of light, and then two glowing spheres appeared over the trees, electricity snarling as they lit up.

"Run," Rodney said.

They ran.

They ran as fast as they could. Men in their seventies were not typically meant to run long distances up winding trails, but the higher they climbed, the quicker they moved, the easier it became. Don didn't really believe that time was running backward, the years peeling away like sunburnt skin. But it *felt* like that. It was as if they had discovered the secret to eternal youth: the collapse of gravity at the end of the world.

As they rounded a corner, something shifted underneath their feet, and the earth split. A long, jagged crack formed between their feet, the side of the trail lurching deliriously. Don yelped as he fell to one knee, skinning the hell out of it. The pain was bright but dimmed almost immediately. Rodney helped him up, pulling him along, the crack continuing on and on and on.

"It's coming," Don panted. "We're not going to make it."

"We are," Rodney growled. "Keep moving."

They did, Rodney's grip on Don's wrist tight to the point of bruising. Up the trail, up and up and up until they crested a hill. Below them, a large expanse of forest as far as the eye could see. The trees looked like they were reaching for the heavens, all their limbs pointed skyward.

And there, sitting on wooden stilts near the edge of a cliff, the fire lookout.

"It looks the same," Don said in wonder. "It all looks the same." He turned. "I remember. I remember him. Shouting. He was—"

He was shouting his joy into the summer sky. He'd never seen anything like it before, the lookout tower. Set atop wooden stilts, it rose high above them.

It'd been Rodney's idea. He'd heard of towers that people could rent out for a night or two. Kind of like camping, but with four walls and a roof. It'd be small, he'd told them. Won't be a whole lot of room for all three of them, but they'd make it work.

It'd been a good couple of months. No fights. No outbursts. No violence. Don thought maybe it was working. That they could be enough. That they could *fix* him. And didn't he hate himself for thinking such things? Of course he did. *Fixing* implied something was broken, and he couldn't bring himself to think that. Their son wasn't broken. He just needed time. Patience. Love. With that, anything was possible.

"Do you see that?" Jeremy cried, jabbing a finger toward the tower. "Can you *see that*?"

Rodney grinned at him. "I can. And guess what? It's all ours for the next three days."

"Three days," Jeremy repeated. "Which means we get to stay the night tonight *and* tomorrow night?"

"We do," Don said. "And look, see that little building next to it?"

Jeremy nodded, bouncing on his heels. "What is it?"

Don ran a hand through Jeremy's hair. "That's the bathroom. It's called an outhouse. It would be difficult to get plumbing up here, so we'll use that. Back in olden times, before people had bathrooms in their houses, they'd have one of these outside."

Jeremy looked up at him with big brown eyes. "I get to poop *outside*?"

Don sighed. "Of course that's what you took from that."

"Yes," Rodney said. "You get to poop outside."

Jeremy pumped his fists above his head. "Yes. *Yes.* Let's go!"

And with that, he took off running toward the tower, Don and Rodney bringing up the rear. Rodney carried a duffel bag for all of them, and Don had a cooler and a backpack filled with food to last them the next few days. It had been a pain in the ass to lug all of it up to the tower, but worth it, in the end. He'd never seen Jeremy so relaxed before.

"I feel good," he told Rodney as Jeremy began to climb the stairs of the tower. "I feel happy."

Rodney bumped Don's shoulder with his own. "See? Told you. Just needed a bit of time."

"Yeah," Don said. "That's all."

It wasn't, and they'd learn that soon enough, but for now, it was true. He felt a low simmer of excitement as he followed Rodney up the stairs, the wooden steps creaking underneath their feet. It was hot, but not bad. No humidity. No clouds. Just a stretch of a sky so blue, it seemed surreal. And in that sky, the pale outline of the moon, a ghost in daylight.

The interior of the tower had two sets of bunk beds, a twin-sized mattress on each bunk. Windows on all sides. A small stove, a small fireplace. Maps lining the walls and plaques with engraved words about the land, the people, the work the fire tower did. A table in the middle with a large compass and an even bigger map of the area.

Jeremy was already climbing to the top of one of the bunk beds, declaring it as his. As soon as that was done, he was back down the ladder and running around the tower, touching anything and everything within reach.

It was a good trip, the kind that was over before they wanted it to be. Hours spent hiking, taking silly pictures, eating bologna sandwiches with cheap yellow mustard. Fires weren't allowed anywhere except in an old woodstove, but that didn't matter. They could still tell ghost stories, could still make s'mores. And they did. They did all of that and more.

On the first night, after Jeremy had gone to bed, snoring, one arm dangling over the side of the bunk bed, Don and Rodney sat near one of the windows, watching the stars come out over the forest.

Don said, "We're going to make it, aren't we?"

Rodney looked over at him with a lazy smile. "I think we are."

"I've never seen him like this before."

"He's starting to trust us. Bet it won't be too long now before we hear the word 'Dad' come from him."

"You think?" Don asked, aching with it. "What a wonderful moment that would be!"

"I think so. You'll see. It's all going to get better from here."

He was wrong. They had no way of knowing it then, but Rodney was wrong.

It didn't get better. Looking back, it was odd they had ever thought it would. But perhaps that was part of the human condition: always having hope, even when it was hopeless.

He'd come into their lives like a hurricane, swift, unexpected. While so many of their community had been left to die in the eighties and nineties—the so-called gay cancer—Don and Rodney had been part of a movement, one quiet and surreal. Behind the scenes, out of the spotlight, hidden away in shadows.

They, like so many other same-sex couples, had wanted a child. Surrogacy in the eighties and nineties was still a new frontier, prohibitively expensive and fraught with the chance the mother would refuse to give up the child, as was her right. But even if they had found someone willing to carry a child, a gay couple taking the newborn home? Near impossible.

Like so many potential parents, Rodney and Don weren't deterred, even when they were told *no* time and time again, a crushing blow that felt deeply personal. But what they could not know before that phone call came in the summer of 1990 was that social workers *wanted* them. Social workers *wanted* to find homes for as many of the kids under their care as they could. And yet, they were left with certain children, unwanted children. Children who had physical or developmental disabilities. In the system, in foster care, in group homes. Children who were *different*, children who weren't what society deemed as *normal*. Children with Down syndrome, children with cerebral palsy, children with histories of significant trauma. Children born in drugs and violence, children who were never given a chance to just *be* children.

They were rejected by most families. People didn't want a child they thought broken or ill or traumatized. They wanted a pretty girl or handsome boy, tailor-made for their families. Babies were especially popular because people could pretend that the child had come from them.

So then what became of the other children? What became of

the orphaned kids who used wheelchairs or had epilepsy or autism? Children who had been harmed, children who lashed out, children who could be angry and violent? Who would take them?

In that summer of 1990, the phone rang. On the other end, a friend of theirs, a woman who worked with the state. She said she had someone she wanted them to meet. She said she hoped they would be as affected by the story as she was. She knew Don and Rodney had been considering adoption. They'd thought they'd have no real chance. After all, they weren't heterosexual. Homosexuality had only been removed from the list of psychological disorders in 1973. Combine that with the AIDS crisis, and same-sex couples never had a chance.

She said, "I have someone I want you to meet."

Two weeks later, they'd driven to Bangor. They'd gone to a nondescript office building to the third floor. Their friend, the social worker, had greeted them. She'd been excited, but nervous. "You'll love him," she told them. "He's a handful, but I think you two would be so good for him." She showed them pictures, told them stories.

Jeremy. Seven years old. A boy, a small boy with brown hair and brown eyes. Knobby knees. Skinny arms and legs. Scars, so many scars. On his back, on his chest, on his shoulders. Scars from other people. Scars from violence.

And a long list of diagnoses. Post-traumatic stress disorder. Attachment disorder. Traits of autism, but that could be a symptom of oppositional defiant disorder. Antisocial behavior. Basically, she told them, it boiled down to this: The boy had been through the wringer. He had survived, but not wholly intact. He was quick to anger. Didn't like authority. Easily irritated. Resentful. Argumentative. Defiant. Vindictive, something that Don thought no child should ever understand. Cruelty through words and actions, even if the intent wasn't there. "Long story short," she told them with a trace of sadness, "he's an angry kid. He'll need a lot of support. I won't lie to you: This won't be easy on any of you. You might even regret ever taking this meeting if things should progress."

Confused, Don asked, "Why does it sound like you're trying to talk us out of this?"

She shook her head. "I'm not. I swear I'm not. It's just that you need to be prepared. Bringing a child into a home changes everything. But when you have a child with the issues Jeremy has, that change increases exponentially. Jeremy might not ever be able to lead a so-called *normal* life. Kids can grow out of ODD, but some don't. And given Jeremy's history, it could lead to other things."

"Like?" Rodney asked.

"Schizophrenia," she said bluntly. "The research isn't there yet, but from what I could gather, Jeremy could potentially develop schizophrenia as he gets older. There will be symptoms to watch out for, symptoms that you might think are part of his ODD or of a potential autism diagnosis, but you need to be aware."

"Has he been in a home before?" Don asked, mind racing.

She shook her head. "Not for any length of time. He became a ward of the state at the age of five. Mom was abusive. She overdosed. Dad was abusive, now in jail serving thirty years for armed robbery. Jeremy has been a ward of the state ever since." She sighed. "He . . . didn't do well, in the foster homes. Many people who foster are some of the kindest and most empathetic people you'll ever meet. Some, though. Some are in it for the monthly checks from the state. Others have too many children already, and it makes it hard to have individual care." She hesitated. Then, "He has hit people. His fosters. Other people in the house. He's punched holes in walls, kicked in doors. He's even taken a swing at me a few times."

"And you think that will make us want to take him in?" Rodney asked.

"No," she said. "I don't. Because that would scare the living daylights out of most people. If you're worried, good. But all of these things we've talked about, everything I've mentioned, it's only part of the whole. Is it a big part? Yes. But I know him. I know him very well. He's curious. He's smart, even if his schoolwork doesn't always reflect that. He can be funny, especially when he's feeling comfortable. He likes to read, even though he has trouble with some of the words. He likes ice cream, especially chocolate. Cats. Blueberries. Climbing. Pretending sticks are swords. He's a child, guys. A child who has been through more than most people see in a lifetime. A child who hasn't really gotten the chance to *be* a child." She looked at them both. "He needs a place to feel safe, a place he knows isn't temporary. I think if he has that, he'll blossom. But again, it's going to take time, patience, and more hard work than you can even begin to imagine. I know you aren't making this decision lightly, but it's better to understand what you're getting into. I don't want to give you any false hopes."

She left them, then, telling them she wanted to give them some time alone before she took them to meet Jeremy. She hadn't told him they were coming, just in case they decided to back out after hearing from her.

They didn't.

The conversation lasted maybe three minutes. Don said that it would be hard, not just on Jeremy, but on them too. Were they ready for something like that? They'd been wanting to have a kid for a while now, and this was the farthest they'd gotten.

Rodney said he didn't know, but that he wouldn't know unless they tried. Could they walk away from this now? Could they really stand up and walk out of the building and drive home and pretend nothing had happened?

"We don't owe him anything," Don said, trying to play devil's advocate.

"Not yet," Rodney said, and that was that.

When their friend came back, she knew from the moment she saw their faces. She smiled at them. "You want to meet him?"

She took them to a small room. Inside, there was a container filled to the brim with toys, some in better condition than others. Colorful plastic blocks, little toy cars, stuffed animals, a Speak & Spell machine, orange and yellow with blue buttons and a black screen. A See 'n Say toy with different types of farm animals on it: *The cow says moooo.*

And the boy, of course. The boy sitting in a little chair. He wore shorts and a shirt with a picture of Mickey Mouse on it. The collar was a little stretched, hanging down almost like a V-neck. Don and Rodney would learn the boy pulled on his clothes when getting worked up. In his hands, a picture book that Don recognized immediately: *Where the Wild Things Are.*

The boy looked up at them with suspicion, seemingly incapable of smiling. Don didn't blame him for that. They were strangers and he didn't yet know whether or not they were the type of people he'd known in his young life, the type of people who caused harm.

"These are friends of mine," the social worker told Jeremy. "Told them all about you, and they wanted to meet you. This is Don, and that's Rodney."

The boy turned back to his book, flipping through the pages.

Rodney said, "Hi, Jeremy."

Don said, "It's nice to meet you, Jeremy."

The boy didn't speak.

"What are you reading?" the social worker asked.

"A book," Jeremy muttered. "I like the pictures."

"It's one of my favorites too," Don said.

It wasn't magic, this moment. Jeremy didn't suddenly look up at them with a smile and tell them he'd been waiting for them. He didn't say much at all during that first meeting. When he did speak, it was in short, staccato sentences. He never looked them in the eyes. When they got too close, he cringed away from them.

That night, sleep was a lost cause. They stayed in bed, but neither slept. Instead, they talked and talked. About what they wanted. About their futures. About why they had decided to have a kid in the first place. About what their lives would be like if they decided to take him in. How everything would change, and it could not be undone. By the next morning, they were exhausted, but resolute.

They went back to see Jeremy again, a few days later. He seemed surprised. He didn't open up any more than he already had, but he also didn't ignore them. The book—*Where the Wild Things Are*—seemed to be his favorite. He could read, he told them. He just had trouble with some of the words. He didn't want to show them right then. Maybe someday, he told them.

The first night he'd stayed at their house—"A sleepover," the social worker had called it—went as well as could be expected. Jeremy eyed the spare bedroom for a moment—fresh sheets on the bed, a green beanbag, some books and toys in plastic buckets—before dropping his backpack and rushing to the window, looking out at the large tree that grew outside. He gripped the windowsill, head turning side to side.

"What do you think?" Don asked, he and Rodney standing in the doorway.

Jeremy didn't look at them. He said, "It's all right. Can we have food? I'm hungry."

That first night, Jeremy didn't want to go to bed. He wanted to play with his toys. When Don and Rodney told him the toys would be there in the morning, Jeremy glared at them with such animosity that it made Don take a step back.

"Do me a favor, yeah?" Rodney said, voice even. "I know it's not the greatest, but if we go to bed now, we'll be able to have waffles in the morning."

That gave Jeremy pause. "Waffles?" he said, the anger draining from his face. "With peanut butter on them?"

They didn't have any peanut butter in the house. "Yes," Rodney said.

Jeremy looked at his toys, flexing his hands. "I guess I can do that."

And that was how Don found himself driving to the store at ten at night to buy a jar of peanut butter. He didn't know it then, but it would become part of their routine for years to come. Always trying to make Jeremy happy. Always trying to give him what he wanted, within reason. All in hopes that one day, the chemicals in his brain would regulate themselves in such a way that the boy would be able to grow up, contribute, be a good person. It's what parents did, they told themselves.

Jeremy ate four waffles slathered in peanut butter that next morning. He said they were very good.

It took months for everything to go through. Months of overnights, months of dreading a phone call that would bring them the news that Jeremy didn't want to live with them, or that they'd never give a child to a same-sex couple. Months of hoping, months of worrying, months of seeing Jeremy's growing smile when they visited him. Once, they had him for an entire week, and by the end, Rodney and Don were exhausted. And yet, it was like a drug, like an addiction, wanting him there, in the home. The sound of his bare feet slapping against the wood floors. His overactive imagination as he waged great battles between the Green Man Army and the ThunderCats. The way his face scrunched up when he was thinking hard.

It wasn't love, but it was close. There was a warmth in Don's chest whenever he saw Jeremy. Three months in, and Jeremy hugged Don around the leg, head tilted back, smiling that gap-toothed smile. Rodney was gruff, but kind, and Don didn't miss the first time Rodney had ruffled Jeremy's hair. They'd been outside, tossing a baseball back and forth. Jeremy had made an amazing catch, arm stretched above his head, body twisted. When he'd landed, he'd shouted that he'd *caught the ball, did you see that? I thought I missed it!*

Rodney had grinned and walked toward him, mitt under one arm. "I did see it," he said, his proud voice carrying through the open window above the sink. His hand in Jeremy's hair, giving it a good rub. "We'll make a ballplayer out of you yet."

Just before everything was finalized—Don and Rodney not daring to believe it was real, not until Jeremy was in their home for good—they met with him and the social worker. An important conversation needed to happen, one Rodney wouldn't budge on. Don agreed, but apprehensively. He didn't know what Jeremy would say. How much did he already know? It wasn't as if Don and Rodney had hidden that they slept in the same bedroom.

"Jeremy," the social worker said. "We wanted to talk to you about something."

He was sitting on the floor, toy cars in hand as he crashed them into precarious towers of blocks. He didn't acknowledge them.

"Jeremy," Rodney said sternly. "I need you to pay attention, please. We need your help. The blocks will be there when we've finished."

Jeremy stiffened. For a moment, Don thought he'd continue on as he had been. Small wonders, he turned toward them, eyes narrowed. "What?" he practically spat.

The social worker leaned forward. "Don and Rodney here want you to live with them."

"I know," Jeremy said.

"Do you like their house?"

He shrugged. "I have my own bedroom there."

She nodded. "I know, I've seen it, remember? It's a wonderful room, just your size."

He shrugged again. His hands flexed. His jaw tensed, relaxed.

"It's a different home," the social worker said. "Different than here, different than other homes. But then every family is different. Some have a mom and a dad. Some have just a dad or a mom. Some people have no kids while some have two or three or even more. Different is good because it helps us see how unique we all are."

Jeremy looked back at the blocks with a mournful expression. "What does that have to do with me?" he asked them.

"Do you know what gay people are?" the social worker asked.

Jeremy frowned and shook his head.

"You know how two people can fall in love and get married?"

"Like with rings and stuff?"

The social worker beamed. "Exactly. Now, when you picture a wedding like that, you probably think a man and a woman are getting married. But what if I tell you that it's not just men and women? Sometimes, men can fall in love with other men, and women can fall in love with other women."

Jeremy's eyes widened. "What?" He looked at Don and Rodney. "You're *married*?"

Don huffed out a laugh. "For all intents and purposes, yes, we are."

Jeremy made a face. "You kiss Rodney? Why?"

"Because I like to," Don said as Rodney groaned. "I like him very much."

"Oh," Jeremy said, and Don knew him well enough by now to see that his mind was racing. Maybe he hadn't given it much thought before. Don worried that bringing it to his attention now might make things harder, but he knew truth was important. Jeremy had been fed so many lies over his lifetime that Don and Rodney couldn't bring themselves to add to it.

"Do you have thoughts about that?" the social worker asked. "Any questions?"

"My mom said people like that are bad," Jeremy said. "She said they're all queers."

Rodney and Don exchanged a glance. If the kid thought he could shock them, he was wrong. They'd heard that word from bigger and scarier people before. This was a child repeating what he'd heard. Nothing more, nothing less.

Rodney leaned forward. "You know bad words?"

Jeremy blinked. "Yeah, words I'm not supposed to say or I get in trouble."

"Right. Sometimes, those words come out if we mean them or not. It happens to everyone. So I'm not mad at you, but I need you to know some of those words you just used aren't nice. They hurt my feelings."

"Who cares?" Jeremy asked.

"I do," Rodney said. "Words are important. They can be used like a gun or a sword. To hurt people, Jeremy. Words can hurt, even if you didn't mean for them to. When we hurt someone's feelings, what's the right thing to do? We talked about this, remember?"

Jeremy scowled at the floor. "No," he said.

Rodney shook his head. "We want you to live with us, kid. We want you to live in our home and be part of our family. But if we do that, you need to understand that our family is different than a lot of other families. Different isn't bad, it's just . . . different. Some people don't like it, but they need to learn to mind their own business."

"Those words you used," Don said. "People have called us things like that before. Mean people, bullies. And I know you're not a bully. You're better than that. I see it every time we're together."

Jeremy ignored them, going back to his cars.

Two days. They stayed away for two days, thinking as hard as they ever had. Weighing everything they could think of. Jeremy's past. His present. His future. *Their* future. What if he continued on as he had? What if he never changed? Or was it like deprogramming, in a way, something that would take time? He was a child. He could still learn. He could still have a chance.

They hadn't planned on going back for three days, but then the social worker called them and told them Jeremy was having a meltdown. He was yelling for them. Screaming. Throwing things. Breaking his bed, his toys. The social worker had a bruise on her arm from where he'd hit her.

When they arrived, he tore into them, demanding to know why they'd left him, that they were just like everyone else, making promises and then breaking them. He was sorry, he told them, tears streaming down his face. He didn't mean to use those words, honest. He fisted his hair and yelled at the ground, face splotchy, cords on his neck sticking out.

It took him close to three hours to calm down, to start catching his breath. By the time the worst was over, Jeremy was exhausted, lying against Rodney, head on his shoulders. "I want to go with you," he muttered. "Please take me with you."

Don wondered if there was anyone strong enough to withstand such an onslaught. *Please,* he'd said. *Please take me with you.*

They did.

And it was magic, both light and dark. Sometimes, they had months and months of calm, months of beauty, months of falling in love with a child who was seeing, perhaps for the first time, that things could be good, things could be pleasant and nice and joyful. Months where they'd go fishing or to the movies or the drive-in burger place with waitresses on roller skates. Months where they'd paint Jeremy's bedroom, where they'd sit around the kitchen table and laugh and laugh. Months of Jeremy reading to them, getting better with his words almost every single day.

But those months—those beautiful moments in time—did not last, nor were they the norm.

At school, Jeremy was enrolled in specialized classes. Under the Individuals with Disabilities Education Act, Jeremy qualified for the Individualized Education Program, which catered to those with disabilities. It was strict, but then it needed to be. Different types of homework from the other students. Oral tests instead of paper tests. Monthly meetings, followed by yearly reviews. The people at the school were good, kind. Patient, even when Jeremy was anything but. Did they say anything about Rodney and Don being parents? Not to their faces, but Don saw the whispers behind their hands whenever they arrived or departed.

They received reports. Jeremy did this well. Jeremy did that well. Jeremy listened today. Jeremy didn't listen today. Today, we learned about kindness. Today, Jeremy threw a book at a teacher. His grades fluctuated, sometimes good, sometimes abysmal. But they did not give up.

And at home: Six months after he arrived, he was told he couldn't go outside until he finished his homework. Jeremy didn't want to do homework. He wanted to ride his bike. No, Rodney told him. He had math problems to do, an entire worksheet full of them.

Jeremy had a meltdown. Chest hitching, hands balled into fists, tears in his eyes, he yelled at them that they were stupid, that they were terrible. He hated them. He hated this house, his room. He hated everything. He kicked a hole into the wall. He tried to do it again until Rodney picked him up, pinning Jeremy's arms to his sides.

"*Let me go!*" Jeremy howled, kicking his legs out.

He calmed down, eventually. It took hours. By the time he was asleep, Rodney and Don could barely stand on their own. They sat in the kitchen, staring at the hole Jeremy had kicked into the wall.

They took him to doctors, to specialists, to psychologists and counselors. Most said he needed to be medicated. An antipsychotic, among other things. It would help him, Don and Rodney were told. And with puberty on the horizon—the body flooded with hormones—it might only get worse from here without some sort of intervention.

It did get worse. Jeremy the surly boy grew up into a surly teenager, quick to anger, quick to violence. At the age of fourteen, he'd punched Rodney in the chest, knocking him into the table, hands raised like he was going to do it again. Don had almost called the police, but didn't. This was the nineties, after all. The police were just as homophobic as anyone else. He didn't want to take the chance that a cop would see their home—see two men raising a child—and run the risk of Jeremy being taken from them. Unlikely? Maybe, but maybe not.

Jeremy had calmed down enough by then, and Rodney only had a bruise on his chest. With that, another trip to the doctors, another increase in his medication.

He hated the pills, Jeremy did. He hated how they made him feel, like he was muted. He argued with them ferociously over them, made threats, saying he'd run away and they'd never see him again. Having heard such things from him before, Rodney had nodded toward the front door and said, "You know how to leave."

Instead, Jeremy had gone to his room, slamming the door so hard, the house shook.

Good days. Bad days. Worse days.

There were the best days, too, days where they were on the road in a rental car. Days and weeks when Jeremy's mind was clear or, at the very least, at rest. He wanted to see everything, and so they did their best to make that happen. Oh, the places they went: To Montana and waters so clear, the deep lakebeds looked within arm's reach. To Arizona, standing before the Grand Canyon, the rock burnt red, the air sizzling hot. To the Appalachian Trail, hiking a good eight miles before calling it quits. To Wyoming, the Grand Tetons rising in all their majesty. To Utah, the petrified forest, rocks in impossible hues. To Tennessee and the Great Smoky Mountains, trying to reach the top of Mount Le Conte.

Those were the days when things felt as perfect as they could be. No one talked about pills or school. They turned up the radio, singing along at the tops of their lungs, windows rolled down, hands hanging out in the wind. They took hundreds of pictures—thousands—of Jeremy, of Jeremy and Don, of Jeremy and Rodney, of all three of them with their arms slung around each other's shoulders, mugging for the camera. Jeremy had grown—a skinny boy shooting up like a weed—and by the time he was fifteen, he was as tall as Don, almost as tall as Rodney.

Nights spent in tents or roadside motels telling stories or watching bad television at midnight, even though they all had to be up and back on the road by six in the morning. In Arizona, they bought tamales being sold out of the back of the truck on the side of the road. In South Dakota, they'd gone to the Corn Palace. In Wyoming, they got snowed into their hotel room during a late-April blizzard.

A good life, albeit a difficult one. As Jeremy's graduation neared, Don and Rodney spent many nights in bed talking. About what Jeremy would do. What he'd become. If he would get better. If he would *stay* better. One thing never discussed? Regrets, because they had none. Even when Jeremy was at his worst—his brain aflame, his anger palpable—they loved him completely and fully.

Then Jeremy started stealing from them. Little things going

missing. Items around the house, small at first, then getting bigger and bigger. Money. Pills from their bathroom, old narcotics from when Rodney had thrown out his back. When confronted, he lied to them, telling them he didn't touch their shit, and goddamn, why did they always blame him for everything? Another hole in the wall, this time by a fist. Rodney made Jeremy fix it himself.

Jeremy graduated, toward the lower end of his class, but still. He *graduated*. They went to the event, dressed to the nines. They yelled and hollered when his name was called. They found him with a group of boys in the bathroom, stoned out of their minds.

He moved out during the summer after graduation. Got a small, shitty apartment with two other boys. Got a job working fast food, and Don and Rodney thought, okay, it's a start. He came home a couple of times a week. When he left, they'd search to see if anything had been taken. They hated themselves for doing it, for not trusting him, but more often than not, something would be missing, usually something expensive.

Jeremy didn't go to doctor's appointments. He was eighteen, he told them. A legal adult. He didn't have to do jack shit. Besides, he didn't like doctors. Always poking and prodding and asking questions he didn't feel like answering. And it didn't matter, he said. He'd stopped taking his pills. He didn't like the way they muddled his thoughts, made him feel like he was drowning.

It was one of the few times Don had ever lost his patience. He was fed up, done with excuses. Pacing in the living room, he snapped at his son: "And you think that's a smart decision? To stop taking the medicine that's meant to help you? What are you going to do when you're out in public, and you lose your cool? What are you going to do if you hurt someone when you don't mean to?"

"That's what you think of me?" Jeremy retorted. "That I want to hurt people?"

"*No*," Don snapped. "I don't think that. But you do, Jeremy. You *have* hurt people."

It didn't work. Tough love, the thing they had relied upon as Jeremy grew older, no longer mattered to him. He wasn't a child. He wasn't a little kid. He could think for himself. Fuck them if they couldn't see that. Maybe they shouldn't have adopted him. He'd be better off if he'd never met them. "Do you know how hard it is?" he yelled at them. "It was already bullshit for me, but then I get two queers as parents? *Everyone* knows. And they talk shit behind your backs. You don't see that. *I* do. *Couple of queers,* that's what they call you. You're nothing more than *queers* who—"

Rodney's hand flashed out. Slapped Jeremy across the face, his head jerking to the side. Not a hard slap, but loud in the deathly quiet that followed. With bright, watery eyes, Jeremy brought his hand up to his cheek.

"I warned you," Rodney said in a dull voice. "I warned you about those words."

"You hit me," Jeremy whispered, a tear falling onto his cheek.

"And I hate myself for it," Rodney said. "But I will *not* allow you to speak to your father that way."

Jeremy stood, chair scraping against the floor. He looked at Don. "You aren't my real father." He turned to Rodney. "And neither are you."

He left, the front door banging open.

Rodney sat at the table with his face in his hands.

They didn't hear from Jeremy for over a month after that. Don would drive by his apartment almost every day, hoping for a glimpse. Calls went unreturned. Friends didn't seem to know much about what he was doing, or so they said. Rodney went to his job at the fast-food place, only to be told Jeremy had quit two months before.

He finally called five weeks later. He told them he was in Montana, camping on his own. He didn't know how long he'd be. He'd met some people. He wanted to travel with them. He sounded manic.

"Please come home," Don said, gripping the phone, Rodney leaning his head in to listen. "We miss you."

Jeremy laughed. "You do? Why?"

"Because we love you."

"I was near a lake this morning," he said. "I heard voices in the water. On the other side of the lake, I saw shadows standing, watching me. No one else could see them. I can't ever tell if they're real or not."

And then he disconnected.

"He'll call back," Don said, more to himself than Rodney. "He'll call back."

He didn't. For four months, they didn't know where he was. They checked hospitals, jails, John Does that had been found on the sides of roads. They filed a missing person report at month three, but they only knew where he'd been, not where he was going. And besides, the officer told them, he's legally an adult. He can do what he wants. No one can force him to go anywhere. A smirk on the cop's face: "Maybe he didn't want two dads for parents?"

At the beginning of the fifth month, they came home to find Jeremy leaving the house. Two other people were with him. A man, a woman, both looking unwashed and faded. Jeremy was carrying their television out the front door. The one from the living room.

He smiled at them nervously, eyes darting to the strangers and then back to Rodney and Don. "Hey."

"What are you doing?" Rodney asked.

"These the queers?" the woman asked. She laughed, an obnoxious, grating little sound. The man slipped an arm around her waist, holding her close.

"Where are you taking the television?" Don asked, gobsmacked.

Greedily, he drank Jeremy in. He looked skinnier, bags under his eyes like bruises. His hair was stringy, oily. It didn't seem like he'd eaten a good meal in a long while. The skin under his right eye was twitching involuntarily. It looked like a tic.

It was then Rodney noticed the other car. A piece-of-shit beater. No paint, only primer. And the back hatch was open, filled with stuff from the house. Not stuff from Jeremy's room, no, but Don and Rodney's things. A record player. The Macintosh computer. Tools. An expensive painting that had hung on the wall of their house since before Jeremy. Cuff links, leather dress shoes.

Rodney turned to his son, wearing a haunted expression. Jeremy still held the television, though barely. "Are you stealing from us?" Rodney asked in a flat voice.

"Jeremy, no," Don said.

A myriad of emotions crossed their son's face: guilt, fury, embarrassment. He said, "It's not what it looks like."

"Then tell me what it is," Rodney said. "Because I'll tell you what it looks like. And if it looks like what I think it is, then . . . I don't know what else to do but call the cops."

"Ooh," the woman said as the man snickered. His pupils were dilated, the irises of his eyes thin slivers.

"Fine," Jeremy grunted, and let go of the television. It dropped to the porch, screen cracking as it tumbled down the steps. "Now no one can use it."

"Let's go," the man said. "I don't fuck with cops."

Don almost laughed. Something they had in common.

The woman blew a kiss at them before going to the car.

Jeremy followed them. Rodney grabbed him by the wrist. "Please," he said.

Please.

Jeremy looked down at his hand, lips pulling back over his

teeth. And then he shoved Rodney with his free hand. Rodney stumbled, fell onto his rear.

They didn't see him again for close to a year, during a week of heavy rain that didn't seem to be letting up anytime soon. A knock at the door, and Jeremy was there, soaked to the bone, his eye blackened, lip split. "Hey," he said, looking down at his feet. "Can I crash here?"

They let him in.

He wanted to get better, he told them the next morning. He didn't want to be like this anymore. He wept, his head down his arms. "Why is it so hard being alive?" he sobbed. "Why is it so hard being human?"

They had him admitted. Voluntarily, but they hoped this was the fabled rock-bottom. That he could sink no lower and now would be the time to rise. And for a while, it looked like it could be that way. Ninety days in the facility. A diagnosis of schizoaffective disorder. New and plentiful medications to try and regulate it. Some good, some so terrible it was like Jeremy was a drooling zombie.

He checked himself out on day forty-nine.

He disappeared and reappeared at random. Sometimes only days would go by. Other times weeks. The longest was fourteen months. They'd worry, they'd fret, they'd hope, but they couldn't do much beyond that. It was one thing telling a child that they needed help, it was another thing entirely when it came to an adult. He'd show up sometimes on his meds, and tell them stories of his travels, all the things he'd seen, the people he'd met. He'd be bright and happy, his hair longer and pulled up into a messy bun.

And then there were the times when he'd be manic, lost, speaking to people who weren't there, jumping at every sound as if it were something coming to attack him. He'd sleep for days on end and then disappear again. Sometimes things would be missing from the house after these visits.

It came to a head the day that Jeremy had gone after Don.

He was twenty-six, and though no one knew it then, only had eight years left alive. He'd been at the house for two days, mostly holed up in his room. Don had come home from work to have lunch, and to maybe see if Jeremy wanted to go out for dinner.

When he received no answer to his knocking on the bedroom door, he'd pushed it open.

Jeremy was on the bed, eyes closed, a plastic tube wrapped around his arm, just above the crook of his elbow. A needle stuck out of his arm. On the nightstand next to him, a spoon with burnt tinfoil, and the stench of something like cat urine in the air.

He opened his eyes at Don's gut-punch exhalation.

It's not what it looks like.

It's not a big deal.

Everyone does it.

I'm not an addict.

I can stop anytime I want.

It makes me feel better.

It clears my head.

Jesus fucking *Christ*, why are you always on my ass?

I can do whatever the fuck I want.

This is *my* room.

"This is *my* house," Don replied in a shaky voice.

Without warning, Jeremy shot up from the bed. Skinny, but taller than Don. Jeremy put his hands around Don's throat and shoved him against the wall again and again and again, head hitting plaster hard enough to crack. Dazed, Don slumped to the floor as Jeremy let go.

"Fuck you," he heard Jeremy say in a low voice. And then he was gone.

Rodney found Don sitting in the same place when he came home a few hours later. When he saw the hands-and-finger-shaped bruises around Don's neck, he bellowed in rage, tearing through the house to see if Jeremy was still somewhere inside. He wasn't. By the time he came back to Don, Rodney was already on the phone, calling for emergency services.

Don didn't want to go to the hospital, but Rodney wouldn't hear of it. Luckily, Jeremy hadn't done much damage, aside from the bruising. Don would have a sore throat for a good while, and the bruising would take time to fade. The nurse in the ER asked him if he was being abused.

When they got home late in the evening, Rodney said, "Never again."

"He's our son."

"He is," Rodney agreed. "And I love him. You know that. But never again, Don. I won't put us in this position again."

They changed the locks on the house. Got a security package: cameras, door sensors, the whole works. They hated themselves for it, more than Don thought possible. This was their *son*, the boy they'd adopted, the boy they loved with everything they had and had given a home to. How could it have come to this? They didn't have an answer to that, at least not one that held any merit. Blaming themselves seemed easiest, and they did that in spades. Maybe if they'd gotten him in to different, better doctors. Or maybe if they'd been stricter when he was younger. Different teachers. A different school. *Something.*

Maybe, maybe, maybe: all the roads not traveled, the ones where Jeremy was happy, carefree, making something of himself. The ones where he didn't feel like his brain was on fire. The ones where he grew up and graduated and found his place in the world. Maybe a wife or a husband. Children, one day, children that Don and Rodney could dote on in their later years.

But no, no, that wasn't what happened.

Instead, Jeremy died shortly before his thirty-fourth birthday. The last time he'd called—a few weeks before—he'd said he was in Washington state. "You remember that fire watchtower? We stayed there when I was a kid. I think that's when I was happiest. I've been chasing that feeling ever since. Think I'm going to head back up there. See if I can stay, get a job or something."

"We miss you," Don said quietly into the phone.

"Yeah, hey, me too. Can you send money?"

He didn't. He didn't send Jeremy money. Not because he didn't want to. He just didn't know what Jeremy would use it for.

A few weeks later, the phone rang. In the evening, near ten o'clock. Rodney answered. He didn't speak much after that, the blood draining from his face.

And Don knew. Somehow, he knew. Maybe because he'd been expecting this call for years. Every time the phone rang, he wondered, *Is this going to be the call? Is it going to be the one where we realize we didn't do enough?*

It was.

Rodney hung up the phone. He turned to Don. Eyes wet. Mouth trembling. Hands shaking. He said, "Jeremy. Jeremy. Jeremy, he's . . . he . . ."

Don fell to the floor and howled.

A ranger had found him. At a campsite, in his tent. Overdose. He'd been dead for at least a couple of days, skin pale and cool to the touch. Nothing could have been done. It was already too late.

They viewed the body in the morgue of the small hospital, the medical staff quiet and respectful. He looked . . . he looked like Jeremy. The body did. An empty space where a soul like a dying star had lived. Don held his hand, kissed his forehead, told him he was sorry, so sorry, that he didn't know it was this bad. He said they should have done more, they should have forced him into getting help, they should have made him do all the things he didn't want to do.

And then the police showed them the letter.

It was short, with scratchy, frantic writing.

It read:

> I'm sorry about this. I don't know how to make it stop. I've tried everything. I don't like myself. I don't like who I am. I hear things. I see things. They tell me I'm awful, that I don't deserve anything good. Maybe they're right. It's so hard being human.
>
> Tell my dads I love them.

Death by suicide, they were told. Suicide by overdose. And didn't that beat all? Didn't *that* just crush them more than they thought possible? It did. It was one thing to live longer than your child. It was something else entirely to find out your child had taken their own life far from home. A mile from the watchtower, the one that Jeremy had once exclaimed in delight over.

It flattened Don and Rodney under the weight of it all. There were long stretches when it felt like they couldn't breathe. Grief like a tsunami crashed over them, dismantling everything they'd built.

They had Jeremy cremated. In clear moments, few though they were, Jeremy had said he didn't want to go into a hole in the ground, didn't want to be food for worms. "Burn me," he'd told them at age twenty-three. "Burn me until there's nothing left but ashes."

So that's what they did. And when they were given the box of ashes, Don couldn't believe how light it was. How an entire universe of a person could fit into a small box as if it were nothing. It wasn't fair. None of it was.

But they listened. Even with all he'd put them through, even with all the bitterness and heartache, Jeremy was still their son. They took his ashes and divided them up into seven different vials. They went to Montana and spread his ashes near the shore of a lake. They went to Arizona and threw ashes into the Grand Canyon. They went on the Appalachian Trail. Eight miles in, they left part of Jeremy under an old-growth tree covered in moss. They traveled to the Grand Tetons in Wyoming, standing on a cliff's edge, letting Jeremy drift away in the wind. They went to Utah, the petrified forest. They laid Jeremy to rest near a stone in the shape of a bird. They traveled to Tennessee and the Great Smoky Mountains, all the way to the top of Mount Le Conte, where they built a cairn of rocks, leaving Jeremy spread around it.

It took them years to do this. Years where the grief sometimes felt like it was fading, only to come roaring back with a gaping maw and sharp fangs, ready to sink into tender flesh. Years of leaving parts of their hearts in places that meant so much to them all.

They couldn't bring themselves to spread the last of his ashes. It would mean the end. It would mean Jeremy was really gone. At least with his remaining ashes, they could pretend. Jeremy was far away, but he was all right. He was healthy. He was happy. He was seeing the world because *that's* what he should have been doing.

So they kept the last of his remains, not ready to let go, not yet.

And then the end of the world began.

They clung to each other, below the fire tower, the earth trembling beneath their feet. Above them, the broken moon, two large chunks pulling away from the fractured body. The black hole was coming. It was almost here.

"We were good parents," Rodney whispered in his ear. "We did our best. It wasn't good enough, but we *tried*."

"We did," Don agreed into his shoulder, shaking. Because that was the truth, wasn't it? They had tried their best. They had still failed, yes, but oh, had they tried.

Rodney pulled back, gripping Don's shoulders. "We did. And now it's time to finish this."

"I'm scared."

"Me too. But we've made it this far."

Rodney was right. They'd survived. Improbably, with all life had thrown at them, they were still here. Don didn't know how that was possible, how he had been able to get himself out of bed every morning, but he had. They both had. And that had to count for something.

Don looked up at the tower. It seemed to be swaying slightly. The air was ozone-sharp, like an electrical storm was approaching. He said, "Let's go. We need to—"

The earth rolled beneath their feet, a fierce tremor that caused Don to stumble to his knees. He looked down at the ground in horror as a large crack appeared between his legs, the earth shifting with a spectacular groan. And for a moment, didn't he think he saw *light* down in the crack? A bright light that looked as if the earth was bleeding? He did.

Rodney grabbed his hand tightly. Before Don could speak, Rodney jerked him up. For a moment, Don felt weightless, going up and up until Rodney pulled him back down. "Go," he said. "Quickly."

They did. They ran as fast as they could toward the tower. The earth continued to shake and shatter beneath their feet. Climbing up a trembling path, Don heard an electrical snarl from behind him. Glancing over his shoulder as Rodney pulled him toward the tower, Don saw ball lightning rising from the cracks in the ground. A dozen balls, all blue and white, crackling, snarling. They rose slowly, arcs of lightning snapping off.

They reached the bottom of the tower as a section of the cliff face opposite the tower collapsed, a loud roar of rock and dust. The plume rose like a mushroom cloud as they began to climb the wooden steps. The tower swayed dangerously with each step they took, the wood groaning like a scream beneath their feet.

Onward, upward, climbing the stairs that wrapped around the tower. Had Jeremy done this? Had he come back here and climbed these steps again? Had he thought about the first time they'd come here? Back when things were easier, back when things still made sense. How did that make him feel? What did he think about? Did he cry? Did he smile? Did he feel a sense of peace that lasted only for a short while?

The top of the tower was shuttered, the door locked, but that didn't matter. They didn't need to go inside. They reached the railing that looked out over the valley and witnessed the beginning of the end.

It looked as if the forest was undulating, *breathing* as the ground rolled beneath it. Trees swayed left and right, up and down. Some fell with distant crashes. Through the trees, ball lightning illuminated fleeing animals: deer, rodents, birds.

"Jesus Christ," Rodney breathed at the scene before them. "Oh my god."

Don, too, was transfixed, but then he shook his head. Setting his backpack on the floor, he began to dig through it. Growing frantic, he thought Jeremy was gone, either left in the truck or fallen out on the journey to the tower. He was about to bellow in rage when his fingers brushed against a familiar shape. Hand closing around it, he pulled out the box that held the last remains of their son.

He clutched it against his chest and swallowed past the lump in his throat. The tower swayed as Rodney placed his hands on top of Don's.

"Let me," he said.

Don breathed in. Don breathed out. He nodded.

Rodney gently lifted the lid of the chest. Inside, six empty divots in blue felt. On the far right of the chest, the remaining vial. About six inches long with a cork stopper at the top. Inside, gray ash speckled with flecks of black. Jeremy, their son. The boy who'd needed a home. Rodney was right. They'd done the best they could. It wasn't their fault. It wasn't Jeremy's, either. It was just luck. Rotten, miserable luck.

Don showed Rodney the vial as he stood. "I have him. I—"

Unfair. It was so goddamn unfair, because right as Don held up the vial, the tower lurched to the right, causing them both to stumble into the railing. Don gasped when his elbow hit first, a flash of bright pain rolling up his arm. His hand flexed involuntarily, and the vial fell to the floor, rolling toward the edge.

Failed, Don thought even as he began to move. *We failed him. We failed then, we failed him now. One last thing, and we couldn't even—*

Rodney moved faster. Just as the vial reached the edge of the platform and began to tilt and tilt and tilt, Rodney fell to his knees, hand flashing out. For a moment, Don thought he'd knock the ashes over, but Rodney managed to grab the vial before it fell.

Neither of them spoke for a long minute.

Rodney eventually stood slowly, face pale. "Now," he said in a shaky voice. "We have to finish this now."

And so they did. Here, at the end of their journey, at the end of the world, they did. Standing side by side, shoulders touching. Rodney held up the vial. With trembling hands, Don struggled momentarily with the cork stopper. It finally pulled free with a muted *pop*. Bits of ash clung to the end of the cork.

"Oh, the places you'll go," Don whispered.

"Where the wild things are," Rodney replied.

They hadn't said much the previous six times they'd spread his ashes. Words felt meaningless, empty, compared to all that Jeremy was. No matter the outcome, no matter what had led to that outcome, Jeremy was their son. He was theirs, their own, not flesh and blood but theirs, regardless. All the darkness compared little to the burning fire that had been Jeremy.

Rodney said, "I'd do it all over again. Even if it would end the same way, I'd do it all over again. For him."

"Me too," Don said in a choked voice. "All of it."

Don closed his hand around Rodney's, holding the vial. They did not count. They did not say a word. They just stood there for a moment in a swaying tower. And then, without thinking, they turned their hands at the same time.

The ash spilled out, catching the wind. It took maybe three, four seconds for the vial to empty, and yet, a lifetime passed from the first granule to the last.

And then.

There would be no later to think back on what they saw. There would be no time to ponder, no chance to revel in the mysteries of the universe. But that did not matter because for a moment, a second or two, really, the ash cloud took on the shape of a face, as if someone stood on the other side and was leaning forward.

At the same time, Don and Rodney whispered, "Jeremy?"

A trick of the light? A wish fulfilled? Or was it there simply because they wanted it to be? The smile widened, and then it dissipated, the ash blowing away. They watched it until they could see it no more.

"He burned so bright," Rodney said, arm wrapped around Don's shoulders.

Don wiped his eyes. "We all did. Every single one of us."

"Do you think we'll see him again?"

"I don't know. I hope so."

A bright flash of light in the distance. Too bright to look at. Like the sun had exploded. Like it was time.

Don turned toward Rodney. He leaned his forehead against his husband's. "I don't regret a thing. Not with you, not with him. All of it, every part."

"Look at me."

Don did. In Rodney's eyes, he could see reflected a large wave of fire. It was coming toward them. Would it hurt? Don wondered. Maybe, but only for a moment. But then, that was life, wasn't it?

"Don't look away," Rodney said. "Keep looking at me. There you go."

"I love you."

"Damn right you do," Rodney said. "Don't look away."

He didn't. Of course he didn't. How could he?

"Nothing to fear," Rodney said. "Nothing to fret about. We'll be all right. We'll be fine."

"We will," Don said. "I'm ready. I'm ready to go."

"With me," Rodney said. "Because where you go, I go."

"I wouldn't have it any other way."

Rodney grinned at him. "I love you too."

Don began to laugh. At the absurdity of it all. At the sheer audacity. "I loved being here!" he yelled into the blazing sky. "I loved it! I loved it!"

Rodney joined in, and as the Earth began to break apart, as everything they and humanity had ever known began to end, they laughed. Clutching each other under a shifting sky, they laughed.

And for the last time, a dying world laughed with them.

Acknowledgments

A person I love very much was diagnosed with oppositional defiant disorder while they were a younger teenager. Today (not so many years later), they are happy, healthy, and whole, making a life for themselves. It has taken a *lot* of work, but they are doing it. And yet, I remember the anger they had, the words they used. Their actions. The destruction they caused. They were violent—never to a person, but in *proximity* to people. They punched holes in walls, kicked in doors. Cops were called numerous times. There were moments when I wondered if they would make it. And I heard the heartbreak, the frustration in their parent's voice. The confusion, the fear, the anger. When someone with ODD is in the throes, it can be near impossible to get through to them. The best I can equate it to is this: People with panic attacks know just how ridiculous it is to be told to just *breathe through it*. It doesn't work like that. With ODD, telling someone to *calm down* or *you're making a scene* doesn't get them to stop. It can, at times, just make things worse.

My family member survived. They are thriving. And though life was full of ups and downs, they're much better off than they used to be. They have the tools now to help them, to not let them fall into the same spiral that they had before. I take no credit for their continued success. That belongs to their parent who is one of my favorite people in the world. She did all the work, did what any parent *should* do: love their kid regardless of how their brain works.

To be perfectly clear: people with ODD and/or schizoaffective disorder don't always end up like Jeremy. They *can*, but there are so many more people who have said diagnoses and go on to live their best lives. I know people like that. I know people who have struggled mightily through the lowest of lows and still find themselves coming out on the other side.

With all of that running through my head, I wanted to focus on something in particular, something I think about quite a bit: What if, no matter how hard you try, no matter what you do, what if your best isn't good enough? What if you fail? What does *that* look like, and how do you go on after? What does the guilt do to a person? How does it manifest? That's how this story came to be.

This book exists because of two people, one real and one not: Ali Fisher, my editor, and Lucy Baker-Parnassus.

When I was editing *Somewhere Beyond the Sea* in late 2023 / early 2024, I got into a bit of a back-and-forth with Ali on a line Lucy has in the book. He says something to the effect of "Black holes can't be seen with the naked eye." As any good editor does, Ali double-checked this and wrote a note about her findings. Part of that note contained the words (paraphrased): *There is a one in a trillion chance that a black hole could make its way to our galaxy.*

To most people, those are miniscule odds. And they're right.

But to me, all I could think of was this: *There's a* chance. Things like that spark my imagination like nothing else. It was like a supernova had gone off in my head, and I wondered if there was a story there.

Before I sat down to write, I had to make a decision. Either this would be a huge book following a bunch of different people dealing with the approaching end, or it'd be a little book with a limited point of view following just a couple of people.

I chose the smaller version of this story not because it would have been easier to write (writing shorter stories is *much* harder than writing longer books), but because I wanted to challenge myself. Could I write a shorter book and have it be as meaningful as my longer ones? I wanted to try.

Funnily enough, this story came quicker than most. The initial draft was completed roughly three weeks after I wrote the first words. I was stunned by just how fast this story came. It was not planned. In fact, it screwed up my schedule a bit as there were other things I should have been focusing on. But sometimes, a story demands to be told, and I, as a writer, have no other choice but to follow it through.

All that to say, this book is my editor's fault. Ali was the one who gave me the idea, so if you're sad/mad/exasperated, please direct all your messages about it to her. She can be reached at blahblahblah@hotmail.gov. Just kidding. Don't do that. She already gets enough emails as it is. Also, that email isn't real. Fun!

To Ali: thanks for letting me destroy the world. You are, without a doubt, the best editor I've ever had the pleasure of working with, and I can't wait for you to accidentally give me more ideas that I unleash upon my readers with unfettered glee.

More thanks go to Lynn, Amy, and Mia, my beta readers. They have been the initial editors for my books for a good while now, and know when to call me on my bullshit. For example: The original last sections of *We Burned So Bright* initially had way more gravity hijinks, and all three of them were like, um . . . no. Not like that. So I changed it to no gravity hijinks at all. And then my editor wanted *some* gravity hijinks, so I proudly showed her the original version, thinking, ha! Take *that*, beta readers! And then my editor said, no, not like that, and I was like, aw, shoot. We were able to find a happy medium for it. So to my beta readers: take *that*, kind of! And also, thank you for doing what you do, even when you demand no gravity hijinks.

To my agent, Deidre Knight, who did not know I was writing this book until it was finished (and then I unceremoniously announced it during a meeting with my publishing team): I wouldn't be where I am today without you. Thank you so much for always having my back, and encouraging me to write wherever my brain takes me. Thanks also goes to Deidre's daughter, Riley, for her amazing insight into this story. She helped me add details that made this story that much more authentic. Thanks, Riley.

In addition, I wanted to thank Elaine Spencer with The Knight Agency. She handles all the foreign rights to my novels and is the reason my books have been translated into so many different languages. It is a *lot* of work (especially all the foreign tax paperwork), and Elaine has been watching out for me since I joined the agency. Thanks, Elaine!

Chris Sickels with Red Nose Studio has once again made a cover that's like he climbed into my brain and pulled the images out. I was a little more particular this time around: I wanted a cracked moon to be front and center. I couldn't wait to see how he pulled it off. And yet—just like every instance before when I see his work for the first time—I was blown away. How is it that a single man can have *that much talent*? For fuck's sakes, he *builds* these entire sets to photograph, and I'm just supposed to pretend he's not some kind of God? Bullshit. Chris is God. And I won't hear anything to the contrary. Chris, your art is a big reason people are drawn to my books. I appreciate you to bits. Thanks.

And then there's Katie Klimowicz, who works in tandem with Chris to create the covers. She designs the cover jacket itself. I think I've mentioned before that Katie is *wild*. Why? Because she can *create fonts* just for a book cover! Who does that?!? Katie Klimowicz does. It's not *just* about creating fonts (though that is pretty fucking cool), but also how the full design will look. She is, in all meanings of the word, an artist, and I'm so grateful she continues to work on my books. Thanks, Katie!

What about the interior design? That credit goes to Heather Saunders, who makes everything look pretty when you open the book. Seriously, these are some unsung heroes that you probably don't even consider when opening a book. You should! These books aren't put out in a vacuum, and so many people put their little touches on them. Thanks, Heather.

Saraciea Fennell is my publicist on the US side of things and works her butt off to ensure that when I release a book, everyone knows about it. You see me at events? That's because Saraciea worked behind the scenes to get me there. Planning book tours is no easy task as there are *so many things* to consider. I know without a doubt that I could not do what she does, at least not without losing my mind. And on top of that, she edits story collections of BIPOC authors such as *Wild Tongues Can't Be Tamed* and *The Black Girl Survives in This One.* They are wonderful collections with dynamic stories from authors who should become household names in the near future. Thanks, Saraciea.

In addition to Saraciea, my publicity teams consist of Khadija Lokhandwala and Sarah Reidy. They handle much of the day-to-day planning, and my career would most likely be an interminable mess without them. Khadija especially gets a bunch of emails from me weekly, and she hasn't yet blocked me. So. That's good.

On the UK side of things, Jamie-Lee Nardone and Stephen Haskins handle my publicity through Black Crow PR. I have worked with them for a few years now, and I'm so chuffed (see what I did there, Brits?) they love books as much as I do. All those online events I do in the UK (and the rare trips I make across the pond) are set up by them. Sometimes, publicity's role can feel kind of thankless as their work is done behind the scenes. But trust me when I say that without them, everything would be a disorganized mess and I'd probably be lost in Manchester, getting my phone stolen again. Jamie-Lee and Stephen are exceptional human beings.

Dianna Vega is an assistant editor and handles so much of the day-to-day of what I do. She is the devil in the details (more Lucy Baker-Parnassus than Satan) and makes sure I'm on top of things. Which, to be fair, isn't always the easiest thing in the world. If I have questions (which I always do), she's the one with the answers. Thanks, Dianna.

The marketing team—Becky Yeager, Tiana Tolbert, Emily Mlynek, Eileen Lawrence, Anthony Parisi—handles all the work in getting my book into the public consciousness. They are tireless people who manage to pull off minor miracles that I don't quite know if I deserve. If you've ever seen official artwork for a novel of mine, or playlists I've put together (or any other promo), it's because they've had the ideas for it. Thanks, all!

The managing editor is Rafal Gibek, and the production editor is Ryan T. Jenkins. The production manager is Steven Bucsok. The editorial directors are Will Hinton and Claire Eddy. The president is Devi Pillai. Who are these people? I call them the bigwigs. They are the reason my books are released at all, and I'm so grateful they took a chance on me all those years ago. I'm at a point in my career now that I can write whatever I want, and they gave me the opportunity to do that. Thanks!

The Macmillan Audio team contains some of my favorite people. The work they do on my projects is collaborative, and every audiobook they release feels like an important little treasure. And thanks also goes to Kirt Graves, the narrator for the audio of this story. I've known Kirt for a decade now, and when he's not making people cry over werewolves, he's making fun of me to ensure that my ego doesn't get out of control.

And thanks goes to Kip S. Thorne, who wrote the Nobel Prize–winning book, *Black Holes and Time Warps: Einstein's Outrageous Legacy*. I read that book in preparation for writing this novel. While it's possible black holes don't work *quite* as I've shown in this book (fiction is, after all, fiction), it's wild to me that we know so much about black holes while still knowing so little. Space is awe-inspiring and terrifying in equal measure. That being said, Thorne's book was written in the nineties and much has changed in the study of black holes since then. To that end, I also read *Black Holes: The Key to Understanding the Universe* by Brian Cox and Jeff Forshaw, two professors who not only made the book knowledgeable but also fun to read.

Also, I have learned that I wish I was good at math, because math is literally the building blocks to *everything*. Younger readers, please take your math classes more seriously than I did when I was your age. Trust me, the universe makes a strange bit of sense when math is involved.

Lastly, to you, the reader: thank you for continuing to support my work wherever my weird brain takes me. I promise the next book won't punch your feelings quite as hard. Or maybe it will because I'm just that kind of author. My bad.

About the Author

TJ KLUNE is the *New York Times* and *USA Today* bestselling, Lambda Literary Award–winning author of *The House in the Cerulean Sea*, *Under the Whispering Door*, *In the Lives of Puppets*, the Green Creek series for adults, the Extraordinaries series for teens, and more. Being queer himself, Klune believes it's important—now more than ever—to have accurate, positive queer representation in stories.

TJKluneBooks.com
Instagram: @tjklunebooks